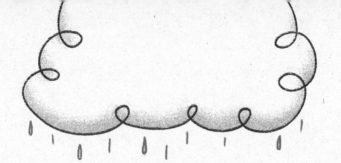

The Death and Life of Benny Brooks

sort of a memoir

The Death and Life of Benny Brooks

sort of a memoir

WRITTEN AND ILLUSTRATED BY

ETHAN LONG

Christy Ottaviano Books

LITTLE, BROWN AND COMPANY

New York Boston

Christy Ottaviano Books
Hachette Book Group
1290 Avenue of the Americas, New York, NY 10104
Visit us at LBYR.com

First Edition: October 2023

Christy Ottaviano Books is an imprint of Little, Brown and Company. The Christy Ottaviano Books name and logo are trademarks of Hachette Book Group, Inc.

The publisher is not responsible for websites (or their content) that are not owned by the publisher.

Little, Brown and Company books may be purchased in bulk for business, educational, or promotional use. For information, please contact your local bookseller or the Hachette Book Group Special Markets Department at special.markets@hbgusa.com.

Library of Congress Cataloging-in-Publication Data
Names: Long, Ethan, author, illustrator.
Title: The death and life of Benny Brooks : sort of a memoir / Ethan Long.
Description: First edition. | New York : Little, Brown and Company, 2023. |
Audience: Ages 9–14. | Summary: Fifth grader Benny wants to focus on not flunking out of fifth grade, but he must also cope with his complicated home life with newly divorced parents, a mother who moves away, and a father with terminal lung cancer.
Identifiers: LCCN 2022062137 | ISBN 9780316333122 (hardcover) | ISBN 9780316333320 (ebook)
Subjects: CYAC: Family problems—Fiction. | School—Fiction. | Cancer—Fiction. | LCGFT: Novels.
Classification: LCC PZ7.L8453 De 2023 | DDC [Fic]—dc23
LC record available at https://lccn.loc.gov/2022062137

ISBNs: 978-0-316-33312-2 (hardcover), 978-0-316-33332-0 (ebook)

Printed in the United States of America

LSC-C

Printing 1, 2023

For the powers that be—
whatever they are

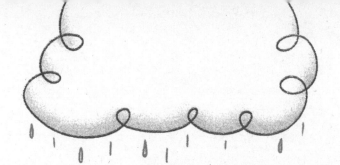

The
Death
and
Life
of
Benny
Brooks

sort of a memoir

1

As I lie here in the backyard in the wet grass, I look up at the clouds passing by, and for a minute, I wonder what it would be like to be dead. Don't get me wrong, I've loved being alive for the last ten years, but lately, it feels like a part of me has died. The part of me that used to be happy and funny and smiley is gone. I think it's because my parents got divorced over the summer. I've been having a hard time concentrating and sleeping.

That's why I like to come outside and lie in the grass. I look up at the clouds and think about sprouting a pair of wings and flying far away. My grandfather died and he's up in the clouds, so it can't be all that bad.

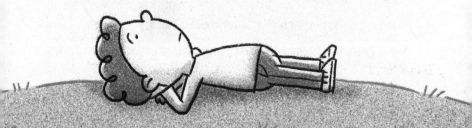

Not long ago, my mom moved away from us. One day she sat us all down and said something along the lines of

I won't be living in this house anymore.

And then she moved to another house. We've never even been there. When I say "we," I mean, me, my older brother, Jake, and my little sister, Libby.

It's been over a month now and you'd think that Mom would miss us more, and maybe even have us over for dinners...sleepovers...anything. But that hasn't happened. She used to be such a big part of our lives—preparing meals, driving us around. She was good at making macaroni and cheese from scratch, not from the box. She'd bake meat loaf with ketchup. And sometimes we'd have fondue. I loved sticking a big cube of meat on my skinny fondue fork. Then I'd dip it in the special fondue sauce she made, which was so good I could taste it for a week after.

Mmmm.

But there is more about Mom to miss than just the yummy food. There were family game nights, even though I would lose most times, playing Monopoly, Scrabble, or Trouble. Jake and Mom liked to play fast but I've got the kind of brain that can't keep up. Back then, we also watched TV shows and movies as a family, while nibbling on big bowls of salty, buttery popcorn.

I like to lie on the floor when I watch TV with my little bowl of popcorn on my chest. I always eat too much and the salt stings the roof of my mouth, especially after hot fondue, and everyone makes fun of me for it.

Mom and I would sometimes watch movies together, and one time we watched one that was about a football player who was dying and his teammate visited him in the hospital. I cried and my mom did, too.

Then there were the trips to the beach, even though Mom and Dad would yell at each other in the car for most of the four-hour trip, and in the hotel, and at dinner.

The more I think about the life we had before Mom left, the tenser I get, and right now, I can't help but close my eyes, squish my eyelids together, and breathe heavily because it's all too much and I can't help but feel angry and sad at the same time. So I swallow it all down. That's the easiest thing to do. Until it floats up again.

"Benny!"

It's my dad. Even with my eyes shut, I can tell he's in a good mood.

"Time for dinner."

I roll to my stomach, really slowly, and push myself up to my knees.

"What are we having?"

"It's a surprise," he says, like he's about to show me the best magic trick ever.

Hmmm. I wonder what the surprise is.

Chicken that's burnt on the outside and bloody on the inside?

Boxed macaroni and cheese with half-cooked pasta and runny sauce?

SPLAM® Sandwiches?
(SPLAM® tastes vaguely like ham if it was spooned out of a dog food can.)

As I clean the grass off my clothes and walk toward the house, I look up one more time at the sky. Clouds pass by. They feel dark, and it looks like they're following me.

When I get in the house, Libby is putting out the napkins and Jake is handling drinks. My job is silverware, which will be easier tonight, because I look at the stove and Dad has cooked up his number one most famous dish to date. The one he gets so excited about. The meal he talks about entering into the Best Meal Ever Competition (if there was one).

His world-famous...
CHICKEN CORN SOUP!

It's the best, and I can say that honestly since I've eaten it a thousand times and never get sick of it. It's got chicken, of course, and corn. But it's got other doodads in it like potato cubes, tiny bits of carrots, slices of celery, and whatever else he uses to make the broth.

"Get ready for my best batch ever!" He scoops a ladleful and holds it up for us to see.

"Look at those rivels!" he says with a huge smile.

Rivels are eggs, flour, and salt all mixed together. Then you drop the mixture into the hot soup and they turn into what amounts to little chewy dumplings.

Dad starts scooping the soup into our bowls, but then...

When my dad coughs, it's like time stops, and everyone who happens to be in the room freezes and waits to see how long it will last. They wait because they wonder if these are going to be my dad's final breaths, if the last twenty-five years of smoking cigarettes are finally going to catch up with him.

Normally, his face turns red and his eyes tear up. Then someone reaches out to pat his back, thinking that will help, and he pushes their hand away. Finally, after about forty-five seconds, he sputters and everything is fine again.

"Whew, I'm okay."

But I don't believe him.

"I swallowed down the wrong pipe!"

Which is what he says every time, and that's roughly about once every other day.

Libby, Jake, and I sit down at the table as Dad scoops the rest of our soup into the bowls.

I bite into a rivel and it feels overcooked, so I'm already searching for chunks of chicken.

"So, how was everybody's day?" Dad mumbles through a mouthful of hot soup.

Jake doesn't answer.

Libby shrugs her shoulders.

Dad looks at me and dabs his chin with a napkin.

"How about you, Ben?"

I pause for a few seconds to fish for corn, then answer him. "Good."

"Well…good is good."

And that was that. He didn't dig deeper.

"Stop slurping your soup!" Jake growls.

I finish my whole bowl, even the last tiny potato cube in the bottom. Then we all clean up the dishes.

"Dad?"

"Yeah, Ben?"

"Remember you said we'd go bowling?"

"Oh, yeah, yeah, yeah." Not making eye contact. "Don't worry, we'll go soon."

It's clear to me he's blowing smoke because:

1. He's just saying this to get me off his back until the next time I ask.
2. I can smell the actual smoke from his breath blowing in my face.

So I drop it.

As Dad is loading the dishes into the dishwasher, his cigarette looks like it's defying gravity. It's stuck to his bottom lip and the ash is seconds from dropping off.

Luckily, he catches it just in time and taps the ashes into the sink.

"Yes, bowling would be good," he says out loud. Now I think he's just filling the air with words.

Soon Dad and I are the only ones in the kitchen. I clean off the table as Dad wipes his eyes from another coughing fit. Then he starts the dishwasher and hangs up the dish towel inside the door under the sink. As he turns to leave the kitchen, he rubs the top of my head, looks into my eyes, and smiles. Then he clicks off the overhead light and disappears around the corner.

All that's left is me standing by the sink with a big black cloud passing by outside and the glow of the sink light as my guide.

2

For the record, I like to draw. If I had a pen and a stack of paper, I would do it all day long. Funny faces, funny sayings, funny animals: Sometimes I'll just draw random objects—an eyeball, a fancy question mark, a Martian with three heads.

I guess it's just how my brain works. It's hard for me to concentrate, so I bounce around from idea to idea, never settling on one. It used to be easier for me when I was younger. Back then, I could draw a whole scene.

You know the one. It's the image of the grass scribbled along the bottom portion of the paper,

and a house with a front door and two windows. Then everyone in the family is lined up in the yard facing out with their arms at their sides and big smiles on their faces. They're standing next to a giant flower, or a tree with a squirrel hole in it, and the clouds are white and puffy and the sky is blue. It's always blue.

Yeah, it was easier to have full thoughts when I was little, when life was sunnier and happier.

Nothing lasts forever.

Jake jumps through the doorway. He loves leaping from behind walls and hidden spots and scaring me when I least expect it. It's his talent.

Before I can get away, he jumps on me, and because he's stronger than a cyborg, there's nothing I can do except try to fight back. But it doesn't work. Before I know it, I'm on my back and he's straddling me so my arms are pinned down and I can't move.

Then he looks at me with the kind of expression that a movie villain has when something thrilling is about to happen. His eyes roll back into his head and he starts snorting and snarling from his nose like a T. rex.

It echoes all over the house and down the hall-way, and I'm surprised the entire world population doesn't hear it, but maybe they do. Either way, it's a long and wet snort, and the whole time he's snort-ing I can see the excitement building in his eyes.

Then when the snorting stops, he starts filling up his mouth with spit, but not just any spit. It's the kind of spit that actually isn't spit at all, but what sounds like the most globby, gooey snot ever. Scientists would want to study it, but they'd have to wear hazmat suits and use tongs just to get near it.

And then my heart stops, because he's pucker-ing up and leaning over my face. The snot appears between his lips, and it's a color that's never been seen in a natural environment.

It's green, beige, purple, and orange all at the same time, with little channels of blood running through it.

In slow motion, it starts lowering itself toward my face. I fight to get free, but it's no use. When I open my eyes, the glob is as close to my face as it can get without touching it and my eyes cross as I try to focus on it.

Jake has pushed the physical limits of what can be done with a snot glob. It jiggles. It glistens. It looks like it's actually breathing. All I can do is scream.

"NOOOOOOOO!"

Then it lands.

Right smack in the middle of my forehead.

Jake rolls off me, laughing and laughing like it's the funniest thing that's ever happened in the history of the world.

I feel the anger building inside me. Then my heart races until I feel my heartbeat in my hands. I roll up off the floor and punch him in the arm as hard as I can.

WHAM!

GET OUT!

"Whoa! Chill!" Jake says. "I was only joking around!"

My face is red, like a hot tamale.

For the record, I have really strong vocal cords. I could be a professional screamer if I wanted, or sing for a death metal band. Jake gets up off the floor and walks out. "What a spaz!" he yells.

I lie there for a minute, then remember there's a hot glob of snot on my forehead, and it's starting to ooze down the side of my face.

It took a lot of soap and gallons of my dad's cologne just to get the stink off my face, but I can still smell it and it makes me throw up a little.

The whole event with Jerk makes me tired, so I take a nap.

I love naps, but my dreams can get pretty weird. In some of them, I fly around, high into the clouds, as my family watches me from a dock below. I fly over trees, down through bushes and cracks in windows. In others, I'm late for school and show up in my underwear, and nobody notices.

The dream I have today is one I'll remember forever. It starts with me flying around in the clouds, but then I can see the desert below. I fly down real low, land on my feet, and look around. It's dark outside and the air feels warm on my face.

Out of the corner of my eye, I see something coming toward me. As it gets closer, I realize it's a rattlesnake. I don't run but stand there and watch the snake as it slithers toward me, gathering speed with every second. I fake to the left, then to the right, but the snake is on a mission.

HISSSSSSS!

Then, in one flash of motion, it strikes but misses me. I feel good about my ability to dodge snake attacks but then I look down and see two wounds on my hand.

I start to feel a little woozy and things get blurrier and blurrier, and I fall to the ground. Then I hear the rattlesnake laughing.

And then everything fades to black.

My dream death startles me awake and it takes me a few seconds to realize I'm in my bed at home and not dead in the desert. I lie there relieved, sweaty and nervous.

I jump out of bed and cross the hall to Libby's room. Libby is eight years old. She has a frilly bedspread, a pink lamp, and cute stuffed animals arranged on her bed. Every morning, Libby takes all fourteen of her stuffed animals and organizes them in a group.

Then, when it's time for bed, she takes them off and stacks them on the chair. Every day, it's the same thing, with the same fourteen stuffed toys.

One of the stuffies is Bee. "Bee" is short for "Bay-bee," which is what Libby called her when she was two years old. Six years later, Bee's hair is falling out, she's lost her dress, and she has yellow spit stains on both her arms and torso from Libby chewing on her in her sleep.

"I just had a dream where a big rattlesnake bit me and I died."

"Wow." She looks up at me with surprise in her eyes. "You look really hot."

"I'm soaked. Plus, Jerk loogied me again."

"Jerk" is the name Libby and I gave to Jake. It's the opposite of a term of endearment, and he's earned it.

"One day you'll get him back," Libby says.

"Easy for you to say."

"Yes, it is easy for me to say."

"Jujube?"

She holds up a box of candy, and of course I take a couple pieces.

They are hard to chew. I like jelly beans better, but these were free so who's complaining.

Briiinnng! It's the phone.

Briiinnng!

I make a mad dash out of Libby's room to answer it, but Jake is already ahead of me.

Briiinnng!

He starts leaping down the stairs, three steps at a time. Then he stumbles...

Briiinnng!

...which gives me an opening, so with my quick feet I dance around him.

Briiinnng!

Then he grabs my ankle and I fall and hit my head on the wall.

Briiinnng!

Finally Jake reaches the phone and answers it. "Hello?...Oh, hi, Mom."

They talk for a minute, with Jake saying things like "Wow. Cool." And "Neato." I can tell he's being sarcastic. Then he hands the phone to me.

"Hi, Mom."

"Hi, honey. How are you?"

I say I'm fine, but fine is probably the opposite of what I am.

"Oh my gosh. I just love Arizona. Such beautiful scenery."

She goes on and on about the weather and how the sky is so big and blue against the red rocks. I might be more excited about it if we were actually there on vacation together.

We never went many places as a family, except to the beach once in a while.

Mom says she needs time away after "all your father put me through."

It's always about her. All the time.

But it doesn't mean I don't miss her. I miss her hugs and her perfume. And I miss having her around. And I want to tell her that. I should tell her that. But today, as she goes on and on about her trip, I just let her talk.

"So how are things with you?" she asks.

She catches me off guard.

I think of school and Dad coughing and my snake dream, and it doesn't feel like the right time to bring all of it up. It may never be the right time.

"Good," I say.

"That's great. Well, honey, put your sister on the phone. I love you and I'll call soon when I'm back home."

"I love you, too," I say.

Then I hand the phone to Libby and head upstairs to take a shower. As the hot water sprays against my face, I pretend that it's washing all my cares away, knowing that it'll take more than hot water to make that happen.

3

This is the point in my story where I'm supposed to get out of bed and take on the day with a smile, and have a cup of sunshine for breakfast.

Well, I don't think that's going to happen because I didn't sleep at all last night, so right now I feel a little like a zombie.

Here's how last night went.

I started out on my back with the covers raised to my neck. Then I lay there looking at the ceiling, and in my mind my life started to play like a movie against the white backdrop of the ceiling. So I closed my eyes, but it's hard to fall asleep.

I watched our old dog, Woofie, once. When it was time for Woofie to fall asleep, he just lay there staring into space, then after a while, his eyes closed on their own. It was a funny thing.

So I tried it last night, lying there with my eyes open, until I got tired and fell asleep.

And it worked!

But like always, after a few minutes, my brain woke me up again, and I got a second wind. That's when I start getting creative with my sleeping positions.

None of these ever lead to a good night's sleep, but I try them anyway.

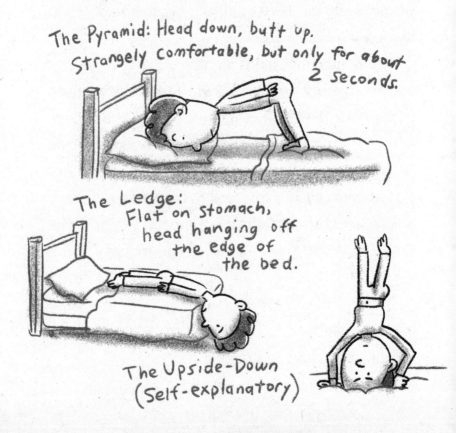

The Pyramid: Head down, butt up. Strangely comfortable, but only for about 2 seconds.

The Ledge: Flat on stomach, head hanging off the edge of the bed.

The Upside-Down (Self-explanatory)

They do serve their purpose, though, because after a few minutes of trying these positions, I'm pooped out.

That's when I get under the covers and make myself a little cocoon. I wrap myself up so just my face sticks out and I make a little face tunnel so I can breathe. It calms me down.

In the summer, it gets harder to sleep this way because it's so hot. To make it worse, Dad doesn't like to turn on the air-conditioning because he wants to save money.

The trouble is I sweat like a hippo and the blanket and sheets get all wet. That's okay because it's better than being awake and restless.

Like I said, today I'm a zombie, but I still need to get up and ready for school. So I peel myself out of bed and don't bother to comb my hair or brush my teeth. I just head downstairs and pour myself some cereal. That's when everyone else starts piling into the kitchen.

"Good morning, all!" Dad says with a gung ho attitude. "Everybody sleep all right?"

Jerk did. Libby did, too. Me?

"Oh, Ben. I forgot to mention…"

Dad has a way of forgetting to mention things.

"You've got a counseling session after school."

—Seriously?

"Your mom and I feel it would be good for you to talk to someone who can help you channel your anger."

Don't they realize they're the ones who need counseling? Mom and Dad fought all the time, so it wasn't really a surprise that they got a divorce. And now that I think about it, their fighting is the reason I started having sleep problems.

Sometimes I'd wake up in the middle of the night to their loud voices, where they sounded like a flute and a tuba having an underwater argument. The flute would shout with a wide range of notes and emphasize with a high pitch, then the tuba would respond with a low, loud note and then a lower, louder note, and that's how it went for hours sometimes.

Lying in bed in the dark made the shouting sound worse. I would stick my fingers in my ears or wrap my pillow around my head, but Flute and Tuba were so loud I could feel them arguing. One time, when it got so bad and I couldn't take it any longer I screamed,

and surprisingly…they shut up.

And for a few minutes it got really quiet.

And I was able to put my pillow back under my head and close my eyes…

Then they would come into my room and say,

We were just having a disagreement.

And they'd seem so calm and collected and warm and loving. It would stay like that for a few days but then the shouting would happen all over again, and that's just how it went.

Dad breaks me from that memory and continues.

"You start this week."

This is the last thing I need right now—to sit with a stranger and share my problems.

"Oh, and kids, I've been meaning to tell you but it never seemed the right time. The doctor found a lump on my lung."

We all freeze in our tracks.

"It's nothing to worry about at this point, but I wanted to let you know I'm going to have a procedure done in the next couple of days to determine how serious the lump is."

And that's where he leaves it.

My dad has a funny way of breaking bad news to us. One time, we had a little dog named Woofie.

Woofie and Dad hated each other. Every time Woofie came into the room and saw Dad, he would growl. Then Dad would growl back. One time their fighting got so bad, they had a standoff in the kitchen. Mom was shouting at both of them to stop. Woofie, with his teeth bared, and Dad, with a newspaper rolled up in one hand, circled around like sumo wrestlers. Dad got in a couple good shots with the newspaper, and Woofie bit Dad's hand a few times. Real soon after that, Dad told us:

Woofie ran away.

And that was that.

Libby, Jake, and I sit silently in the kitchen and eat our breakfasts. Then it's time to head to the bus.

I guess this is my new life: a house without a mom, sleep problems, and a dad who has a lump on his lung.

I look at Jake, then at Libby.

Neither of them seems to be bothered by all that is happening. So maybe I shouldn't be bothered either.

But it does bother me. A lot.

It bothers me like the time I was throwing up really bad in the bathroom. I was sweating and moaning over the toilet and no one came in to see how I was doing. In the morning, I slept until lunchtime and no one came in to see why I was sleeping until noon on a Saturday. They didn't even ask why I was green in the face and looking like I just died.

It stinks when nobody cares or no one wants to be bothered, and that's how I feel about Jake and Libby. It's like all of this isn't even on their radar.

"Have a good day, guys," Dad yells from the kitchen as we head out the front door to the bus. Then I realize I left my backpack in the kitchen, so I go back inside.

I come around the corner and see Dad studying a piece of paper, the kind you get from the doctor with lots of scribbly handwriting on it. He's looking at it and breathing deep sighs. I want to go hug him, but decide to leave quietly instead. I grab my backpack and run out the door.

On the bus I see the same kids I do every day. There's Kirby Smith and Patrick Andersen (whose family is from Sweden, I think) and Johnny and Jimmy McTish and Jesse Hiccup (yes, his last name is Hiccup) and of course Bobby Blankenballer, who always sits in the back of the bus. He likes to make fart noises and curse and act all cool.

I look around some more as I walk down the aisle and see Theo Steinwell, my best friend. He must have gotten on the bus really early because he's waaay in the back and in a deep conversation with Johnny and Jimmy. Luckily, he saved a seat for me. So I slide in next to him as the bus pulls away.

"Hey, Mr. Fancy Hair," Theo says, and then smiles sarcastically. "Did your mom make you comb it like that?"

I give him the evil eye.

"Oops. Sorry. How is your mom anyway?"

"She's good, I think."

But I really don't have a clue how my mom is doing.

Theo gets back to talking with Jimmy and Johnny about cars. He knows more about cars than anyone on earth. He's only ten but could probably work at the factory making spark plugs and designing steering wheels and building hot rod engines and all kinds of stuff.

Theo's dad loves cars, so Theo loves cars. That's how things work, I think.

I'm not really sure what my dad loves except working and cigarettes and sleeping and maybe eating soup. That's about all I see him do.

The bus slows down at the next stop and more kids pile on. Pete Peterson (who names their kid the same name twice?), his brother, Oliver, and little Mikey Avarino, who is really short for his age, walk through the aisle.

Then someone gets on the bus who's been my nemesis since kindergarten.

Betsy Morgan.

Ugh.

She really REALLY annoys me. If you get her going, she just yaks and yaks and never shuts up. She's like one of those windup toys that's just a set of teeth and when you wind it up it yaks for two minutes straight. That's all I think about when I see Betsy Morgan. Teeth yakking.

As she walks down the aisle looking for a seat, she stares directly at me and catches me with a look on my face like I smelled someone's stinky underwear, but it's just how I feel about her and she knows it.

She smiles at me with the fakest smile I've ever seen, then turns and sits down next to Jenny Wolfe. Both girls look back at me and laugh.

There's a ton of noise on the bus. Larry the Bus Driver has the music cranked at full volume. It's so loud, you can't even hear the words to the songs or the guitars or the drums—all the instruments just blend together.

Plus, everyone is screaming and yelling and throwing stuff at each other. Even though Larry the Bus Driver yells at all of them to sit down and be quiet, nobody listens, and that's pretty much how the bus ride to school goes. So I do what I always do on the bus—zone out.

I look into the distance, past Theo, past the bus window, and into the trees as houses and buildings pass by. My mind starts thinking about all the things that are happening and I start to imagine a different life for myself, maybe as a mountain climber or a game show host, or even a gazillionaire. Then I picture myself in a space suit blasting off to the cosmos and being the first astronaut to land on Mars. When I come back to Earth, everyone cheers and interviews me and snaps my picture for the paper.

During the celebration of my successful Mars adventure, I look over and see my dad and mom in the audience clapping. Dad is on one side of the room and Mom is on the other. Dad is sitting next to an air tank with a clear hose up his nose because he can't breathe on his own anymore, and he starts coughing, and then I have to help my dad and everyone is watching him and then everyone is looking at me and Dad keeps coughing and I want everything to stop but it won't, and I squish my eyes together.

"Hey, wake up, Space Case," Theo says, snapping his fingers in my face.

I come back to reality and everyone is getting off the bus in front of school.

"Come on," says Theo as he pushes against me.

I push him back, then grab my backpack and exit the bus.

There's nothing like being trapped in a crowd of kids heading into school. It's sort of like riding the bumper cars. You gotta stay alert and keep one foot on the gas and one on the brakes because you never know when some random kid is going to come flying at you from behind, or sideswipe you out of the blue, or even crash right into the front of you.

I steer through the traffic and head to my homeroom.

Then my day plays out like this:

Math class. Ugh.

Social studies. Mr. Rodgers is the most boring teacher ever.

English. Sort of okay.

Gym class. Why do we have to wear these stupid uniforms?

But then comes my favorite class...

Art.

It doesn't get any better than art class, at least for me.

Mrs. Finnuken has been my art teacher since I was in the first grade. She's in her usual cranky mood.

GET OUT YOUR SUPPLIES AND SET UP FOR YOUR ART ASSIGNMENT!

I get out my paper and colored pencils. I like colored pencils.

I pick a seat closest to the center table, organize my stuff, then finally look up at the subject matter in front of us.

And my eyes widen.

Another boring still life.

There's a fruit bowl and flowers in a vase and a sombrero. Why does Mrs. Finnuken pick such boring stuff?

I let out a sigh and then look around at all my classmates scrambling for good seats and supplies.

Then I see Lori.

Let's just say Lori has a little crush on me, and I don't really like her back. Don't get me wrong, she's friendly and has never said a bad word about anyone. She's in some of my other classes, too, and she always has a good answer and is polite to the teachers. The point is, she's not a bad person, she's just too…well…aggressive.

She looks at me like it's her birthday and I'm the big present in the corner that she can't wait to unwrap.

The worst thing about her is...

She smells like salami.

SALAMI

LORI

"Salami" is not a great fragrance.

She likes to leave little notes with hearts on them in my desk and put smelly stickers on my shirts. Not stinky ones—they actually smell like fruit—but I don't like them sticking on my clothes.

She just makes me feel uncomfortable in so many ways, and I always try not to look at her, but she always catches me looking at her and it probably makes her think that I like her.

But then...

The heavens open up and angels start singing and the Girl Who I Would Love to Have Catch Me Looking at Her just walked into art class.

Every time I see her, I feel like I'm having a heart attack. I think I'm too young to have a heart attack, but it sure feels like one.

Her name is Krista Shotfelder, and she's what I'd call a goddess. She's really tall with shiny, wavy brown hair and cherry-smelling lip gloss.

If Krista put a fruity-smelling sticker on my shirt, I would wear that shirt to bed every night and in the shower every morning and never take it off for the rest of my life.

Unfortunately, she doesn't even know I'm alive and it's probably going to stay that way, knowing myself as well as I do. If she did get to know me, she'd soon find out about Jerk, and my mom not living with us, and she'd definitely hate sitting at dinner with us and having Dad smoke at the table as she tries to eat cruddy hot dogs and cold macaroni and cheese. It just wouldn't be a good thing.

Her love is not worth the risk. So I admire her from afar and go about my day.

On to science class. Ugh.

Maybe I should go back to Mars.

5

"Benny! Get in the car!"

For what?

"Time for therapy. Seriously, we gotta go! Your session is at three o'clock and I have a meeting! Let's go, let's go!"

It's not like I have a choice to go or not go, and Dad would just ignore me anyway or get mad if I don't get in the car.

So I follow directions.

Dad is smoking like a chimney, which is how he normally smokes, but this time he's taking a puff every two seconds. He's also driving fast, which is making me nervous.

We squeal around a corner and screech around another, then pull up to an old house.

"Okay. There you go," he says.

I look at him.

"Aren't you coming inside with me?"

"I told you I have a meeting."

I freeze in my seat and stare at the glove compartment, not wanting to move.

Dad breathes out of his nose and swings his door open and comes around to my side and swings mine open, too. He moves fast for a guy with a what-might-be-a-tumor on his lung.

"Benny. Now!"

I don't want to go.

I squish my eyes together and my heart starts to race and Dad reaches down and grabs my arm to pull me out of the car, when all of a sudden...

"I'll take it from here, Mr. Brooks," says a voice behind my dad.

I look up and see a man walking to the car.

My dad doesn't know what to do except to let go of my arm and say, "Oh, hi, you must be Brian."

"Yes," says Brian, "and you must be Mr. Brooks."

He shakes Dad's hand, then turns to me.

"And you must be Benny."

I look at Brian and give him a half smile. Our eyes lock, and once they do it's hard to look away. His eyes are light blue and deep-set. They aren't like Frankenstein's eyes or anything, but a little scary nonetheless. It feels like he's focusing so hard on my face that lasers are going to start firing out of his pupils.

Now THAT would be scary.

"Come on in and we'll get started." His arm gestures toward the house.

"I'll be back in a bit," my dad says as he pats me on the shoulder and quick-walks to his side of the car. He gets in and pulls away.

I watch the car as it drives around the corner and out of sight.

Then I look back at Brian.

"Looks like your dad is a busy guy."

"Yeah, I guess so," I say, not intent on keeping the conversation going or telling him that my dad has a tumor, or that I'm not really interested in being here and talking about my problems to a Guy I've Never Met.

But he keeps talking.

All the way inside.

He asks me about my brother and sister and how old I am and what school I go to. I keep thinking he's going to ask me what kind of cereal I like or how many times a day I take a shower, or if I eat my boogers (which I don't) but luckily, he doesn't.

Finally, we make it to his office, and I stop inside the doorway. I feel really nervous and just stand there looking around at the inside of the room. There's a brown leather couch and a red chair, a small desk, and a wall of bookshelves with so many books I can't believe anyone would ever read that many. Brian must be smart.

There's also lots of framed pictures of Brian with his family. Oh, and there's a box of tissues on a side table next to the couch.

"Are you all right, Benny?"

I pause for a second.

"Yeah, I'm okay."

He takes a deep breath and lets it out.

"We'll take this slow, at your own pace," he says, with comfort in his voice. "I'm not going to force you to say anything you don't want to talk about."

His words make me relax, but I still feel like my feet are frozen to the floor. Then I think of my dad and how mad he'd be if he found out I didn't go to my therapy session.

So I walk into the room and flop down onto the couch.

Brian shuts the door, then picks up his notebook and pen and sits down in the red chair across from me.

"So when I was a kid, my grandmother died and it really upset me. My mother was especially upset by it, so she thought it would be a good idea to talk about it. She also thought it would be a good idea to take me along with her. At first, I really fought against it. But once I heard my mother talk about things and express her feelings, the weight lifted off her shoulders and she was able to be happy again."

I stare at Brian. That was a lot of words. Now all those books make sense.

"I'm not promising that we're going to get any-where with this and that you'll be happy again."

"I am happy," I blurt out.

He continues.

"All I can promise is that I'll be a good listener, and if you want to talk about something, you can talk and I will give my two cents if you want me to. You are in control of this discussion. Does that sound fair to you?"

He's giving me control? Control over this ses-sion and everything I say and do? It's like he just gave me a superpower.

Maybe I can control his mind and make him start walking around and clucking like a chicken on my command.

BOK BOK BOK!
BOK BOK!
BOK BOK BOK!

Maybe I can make him give me the combination to his safe. I bet there are jewels and gold coins in there.

"Benny, does that sound fair?" he repeats.

"Yeah. I guess so," I say.

I find out really fast that having control is harder than it looks. If I can talk about anything in the world that I feel like talking about, should it be space travel? Or gourmet waffle recipes? Or kangaroos and the art of hopping?

The sky is the limit and I have so many ideas, but in the end, there's only silence. And Brian stares at me, waiting for my mouth to spit something out.

But then it starts to become clear that what I want to talk about won't come out at all.

I want to talk about my mom and what's going on at home and Jerk and my grades and I want to talk about my sister and my sleeping positions and the way I get really, really angry and scream at the top of my lungs.

I want to talk.

But I can't.

It won't come out, and when someone I just met is staring at me with icy-blue laser eyes, it makes things worse, and that's when my blood starts pumping and my eyes start to tingle and I can't stop it...I can't stop it...and my hands clench up and my eyes squish shut and since I am in control of this session and I can do or say anything I want, I do the only thing that comes to mind to bring me relief. I don't even think twice.

I get up, open the door, and run out. Like my shoes are on fire.

Yeah, I run out and my dad is going to be mad and I'm not sure where to go or what to do because Dad is at a meeting.

So I run outside and across the grass and flop down on the curb in front of Brian's house or office or whatever it is. My eyes squish shut again and I wonder what's going to happen next.

After a few moments, Brian comes out and stands next to me on the curb. It's kind of quiet for a minute, but then he speaks up.

"No one has to know."

Brian's words are a relief.

"But I'll trade you. I won't tell your dad if you promise to come back next week."

He's got me. And something tells me it's a pretty good deal.

"Okay. I'll come back."

"Good."

We sit there for a little while and my dad comes back, but he's twenty minutes late.

"How'd it go?" he asks as I get into the car.

"Okay."

"Just okay? Did he figure out what's wrong?"

"I think it takes longer than one session, Dad."

"Well, I hope it doesn't go on too long because these therapy sessions are expensive."

All I can do is roll my eyes to myself and look out the window.

Back home, we have frozen hamburgers and Tater Tots that are crispy on the outside but a little cold on the inside, but still taste good.

"Jake, could you pass the ketchup?" I ask, trying to be nice.

He throws the ketchup at me like a quarterback throwing a football, and it bounces off the table and into my face, squirting all over the place.

"What?!" he says, playing dumb. "You said to pass it!"

Dad whaps him on the back of the head and we all go back to eating in silence.

For the rest of the meal, I can't stop thinking about standing in the open door of Brian's office. Maybe my life is just an open door waiting for me to enter it.

What I do know is that these Tots need more ketchup.

6

"You went to therapy?" Theo asks as he pumps up a bike tire.

"Counseling," I say, correcting him.

"Counseling. Therapy. It's all the same."

I sigh. "I shouldn't have said anything."

"Ha. I'm only kidding, Ben. You have a lot of stuff happening right now. Actually, going to talk to someone about stuff isn't so bad."

"It feels bad," I say.

I sit and watch Theo as he polishes up an old bike he bought from one of the McTish brothers with his saved-up allowance. It's really rusty with big swooping handlebars and a banana seat. It will be pretty cool when he's done cleaning it up. I've seen him do it before. He takes steel wool and rubs it on the chrome to get it really shiny. He says the trick is to use superfine steel wool so it doesn't scratch the chrome. It's working. The chrome is sparkling.

But my eyes keep focusing on his other bike. It hangs on the side wall of the garage. It's white with shiny red lightning bolts on the frame. It's like the hot rod of bikes, the Rolls-Royce of riding. It's one of the best bikes you can buy. I know this because Theo has told me a million times and keeps telling me every chance he gets.

And I want one.

"You wanna ride it?" Theo asks, catching me drooling over his bike.

"No, that's okay."

Theo pauses, then realizes why I'm being so weird about it.

"Oh, right, you don't know how."

He starts smiling, then catches himself.

"Just forget it!" I say, and start looking down at the ground.

Theo takes the bike down off the wall and sets it up in front of me. Then he pushes the garage door button.

As the door opens, Theo is smiling at me and shaking his head.

"I tried when I was little and I went really fast, then fell over and got hurt. I never rode it again," I say.

I look Theo in the eyes, and he shrugs.

"The truth is, my dad pushed me so hard on the bike that I couldn't control it very well and I didn't know how to pedal, and then because I got frustrated and cried, he put the bike in the shed and that was the end of that."

"Well, today is your day to try again."

He holds out the handlebars for me to grab.

I take the grips into my hands and stand there, frozen in my tracks.

"Get on."

After a long sigh, I swing my leg over and it catches on the tire, making me lose my balance. The bike and I tip over onto the ground, missing Mr. Steinwell's car by an inch.

Theo shakes his head.

"This is going to be harder than I thought. Try again, but out here."

I get up and straighten out the bike as Theo looks for scratches. Then I swing my leg over.

This time I'm able to keep my balance.

"Put your feet on the pedals and start pedaling!"

Theo holds me up and I put my feet on the pedals, then he pushes me slowly out of the garage. I roll onto the driveway and pedal, veering to the right, pedaling harder, veering to the left. The handlebars shimmy and shake, and I start leaning to the right. I fall over in the grass.

I look up at Theo, who's standing with his hand over his eyes.

"Okay. Let's try one more time."

He runs into the back of the garage, clinks and clunks around for a few seconds, then comes out with an adjustable wrench.

He starts loosening one of the bike pedals—so loose, in fact, that it comes right off. Then he takes off the other one.

I look at the bike with no pedals.

"How am I going to ride it now?"

"Trust me. My uncle Mike showed me this. He did it for my little cousin."

Theo helps me up and we roll the bike to the driveway. I sit on it again with my hands gripping the handlebars and my butt on the seat. Where my feet will go is still the big question.

"Now start pushing yourself around with your feet. When you feel yourself falling to one side, just stick your foot out and catch yourself."

"That sounds easy enough."

"After a while, you'll start to use your feet less and coast farther and farther in between steps. Then I'll put the pedals back on and you'll be riding."

It sounds too good to be true, but even more, it sounds genius. Theo might actually be a genius. Or more likely, his uncle is the genius.

Theo counts down.

"Ready, set, GO!"

I push myself forward, using my feet just like Theo said. Right away, the bike starts falling to one side, and right away, I stick my foot out to catch myself. Still rolling, the bike starts falling to the other side and I stick my other foot out. The more I roll, the more I lean and the more I lean, the more I stick my feet out. After a minute or so, I'm barely falling to one side anymore or using my feet to stop.

To me, it feels like a miracle.

"Go Go GO!!" yells Theo.

I just keep going and swoop this way, and swoop that way, and start riding.

After about twenty minutes we put the pedals back on, and from that point forward, there is no stopping me. I start getting brave and riding out into the street and swooping left and right and rolling up to a parked car and turning at the last minute to avoid crashing into it.

The cold air is blowing against my face and it feels like I'm flying. Clouds pass by and I hear the wind blowing in the trees and snot is running down my nose. I reach one arm up and wipe it on my sleeve. There's nothing else I care about more right now than riding this bike and feeling the freedom. I want to stay on forever.

"My turn!" shouts Theo, and I see him chasing after me as I ride up the hill. I swoop back down, zipping past him and smiling as I ride down the street.

The cold air. The breeze. The freedom. It's all taking my breath away. I close my eyes and take it all in.

"LOOK OUT!" Theo shouts.

My eyes open to the image of a parked car and before I can blink…

I fly over the bike and into the back of the car and get the wind knocked out of me.

"Are you okay?" Theo says, all worried.

"Yeah," I squeak, barely able to breathe. The bike ride really did take my breath away.

Luckily, nothing happened to the bike except Theo has to straighten the crooked handlebars. It takes me a couple of minutes to breathe normally again.

Back at Theo's house, he asks his parents if I can sleep over and of course they say yes. They always let me sleep over. They're probably the nicest parents I've ever met.

They talk to me like I'm a normal kid, not some idiot who doesn't know what he's doing. They think I'm smart and funny and they like to joke around with me, just like Theo jokes around with me. They're a little older than my parents, so maybe they're just more mature.

Mrs. Steinwell makes meat loaf and mashed potatoes with gravy. My body is still a little cold from being outside for so long, so it will probably feel good in my stomach.

"That's Theo's grandmother's famous recipe," says Mr. Steinwell.

After dinner, we play a game of Scrabble and even though I'm not a great student, I'm really good at making words and getting lots of points. Theo and his parents are good at Scrabble, too, so tonight it's a tight game.

That is, until I pull ahead with the best word I ever put down in a game.

"*Meerkats!*" shouts Theo. "And on a triple word score, too!"

"And I used all my letters!" I add.

"Holy smokes!" says Mrs. Steinwell. "I think that does us all in."

They all high-five me, even Theo, who looks like his goldfish just died. He hates losing.

"You, my friend, deserve something special for that win," says Mr. Steinwell, reaching into his pocket.

"I found this old penny this morning. You know what they say...Find a penny, pick it up..."

I finish the sentence. "...All day long you'll have good luck."

"And you, young man, had all the luck tonight."

"And some skill, too," I say with a grin.

"Yeah, and some skill, too, I guess," he says with a wink.

"Mom Steinwell, would you help me clean this up?"

"Certainly," she says.

Theo and I head off to the loft above the garage, where it's really cold, but really cool, too. It's like our own private hideout. Theo's mom brings us a whole closet full of blankets to lie under and I quickly warm up. "Let's sleep here tonight," Theo says.

"Really?"

"Yeah. It won't be so bad."

Theo and I talk for a little while, but soon the talking gets further and further apart and at some point we stop. I won't tell exactly what we talked about because it's private, but let's just say

it involved a certain girl who Theo likes. Another certain girl that I like never came up, but maybe talking about Krista and her long wavy hair and shiny lips would have gotten her out of my mind because it's really hard to fall asleep thinking about those kinds of things.

But tonight I do okay.

7

Yak. Yak. Yak. Yak. Yak. That's all I can hear. Even though the bus ride home is louder than ever, with the usual yelling, screeching, thumping, and music blasting. It's like Betsy Morgan is a giant parrot sitting on my head, squawking for crackers.

She actually sounds more like a pterodactyl. I squish my eyes together to block it out, but the sounds keep coming at full volume. Luckily, the bus is just a few blocks from my stop, but seeing as how Betsy's voice is taking up all my ear space, it can't come fast enough.

The bus slows down. I have this dream where I take Scotch tape and wrap it around her mouth a million times. The problem with this fantasy is she'd most likely use her yak teeth and gnaw a yak hole right through the tape and just start yakking again, so I'm not sure there's anything I can do to stop her. I'm just going to have to keep suffering through it. I guess I could also walk to school. Too bad it's five miles away.

But all my evil thoughts about Miss Motor-mouth come screeching to a halt when I see Mom's car parked in front of our house.

What in the world would she be doing here?

As Jake, Libby, and I walk to the front door, I hear muffled voices coming from inside and it sounds pretty familiar.

When I walk in, everything becomes loud and clear.

"Yeah, but if you ever listen to me, like you never do, then you'd know to just stay out of my business," Dad yells in Mom's face.

"Your business? You have no idea what your business even is."

"And you have no idea how to be a wife, or a mother for that matter."

"Ha! I raised these kids!"

"Yeah, and then you left!"

"Because of you!"

And it keeps going on like that. I walk over to the kitchen counter. There's a casserole dish with foil over it.

Lasagna. Mmm.

I try to block out their screaming.

Yak! Yak! Yak! Back and forth. That's all it sounds like to me.

What makes it worse is that they don't even notice Jake switch on the TV and turn the volume up really loud to try to drown them out. They just get even louder. And Libby is standing right next to them, making hot chocolate and just going about her business, and they don't even notice.

It's like we're not even here.

"And what kind of idiot has cancer and keeps smoking cigarettes!"

"You know what, when you get cancer, you tell me how you like it. Forget it—I don't have time for you."

"You never have time for anything. You just keep running away like a child. Just like your father!"

The lasagna dish explodes into pieces and turns the whole house quiet as my dad walks off in a rage.

"AND DON'T COME BACK!" he screams.

Mom still doesn't notice that we're home. She grabs her purse and heads to the front door to leave.

I run after her.

She turns as I wrap my arms around her waist.

"Now's not a good time, honey." She pats me on the shoulder, turns back toward the door, and leaves.

I wish my parents liked each other. It makes me sad and mad at the same time that they can't just put their heads together and work things out.

I head upstairs and decide to take a bath, with lots of bubbles, of course, and when I get in, I lean back and sink my head under the water with just my nose sticking out. It's a nice relief from what happened and a great getaway from everything else, too. The water fills up my ears and all I can hear is the dripping of the faucet and the sound of my own farts bubbling to the top.

Other than that, it's pretty quiet.

My brain is bopping around from thought to thought. The exploding lasagna pan. Betsy's mouth. Krista's blue jeans and lip gloss. It's all ricocheting around in my head.

But I also keep thinking about the bike ride.

Theo's bike. Ten-speeds. Even unicycles. There are so many kinds. I think about the kind of bike that I would like, one that I could ride forever and maybe one that flies in the air so I can pedal it high up into the clouds and really get away from everything.

Now is definitely not the right time for this, but I jump out of the tub, dry off, and run to Dad's room with a towel wrapped around me.

Dad?

"What."

"Can I get a new bike for Christmas?"

"Oh come on, Benny, you asked me this before."

"Yeah, when I was five."

"Yeah, and you know how that turned out."

I do know how that turned out. But I keep going.

"Yeah, but Theo just showed me how to ride his. I can do it now."

Dad breathes out his nose, which is not a good thing.

"Benny, I'm just not in the mood right now. I'm exhausted. Just...please go."

And my shoulders sink.

I turn around and walk out of his room.

"Good night, Dad."

"Night."

✦ ✦ ✦

It's really too early to go to bed, so I try digging into some homework.

My mind is racing a mile a minute and it's too easy to get up and find something else to do.

So I draw. Then I read the first two pages of a comic book. Then I pick my toenails.

When it's late enough to go to bed I lie down and as usual, I can't get comfortable and I keep flopping around like a fish in my bed trying to find a better position.

I try "the Zombie," where I walk around with my arms out in front of me to make myself tired.

"The Jelly Bean," where I curl up into a ball for as long as I can.

And "the Mole," where I hide under the covers until there's barely... any... oxyge... left.

Nothing is working. So like usual, I just lie there thinking about things and my mind won't stop and it just gets worse and worse with every minute that goes by.

I can't pinpoint the exact reason I'm feeling so restless, but I can make a pretty good guess that the broken lasagna pan on the kitchen wall has something to do with it.

My dad doesn't talk much to us about his tumor, but it must be getting worse. My mom coming by today was her way of showing that she cares, but she couldn't keep her mouth shut and it backfired and made everything super worse.

I start breathing heavy and panicking and seeing it all again in my head. I just can't lie here anymore.

I spring from my bed and run out of my room, down the stairs, and out the front door.

There's nothing spookier than being outside at two o'clock in the morning when there are no cars on the road or people. It's so quiet. All I hear is the wind blowing in my ears and the sound of my teeth starting to chatter.

It feels about zero degrees outside and I didn't stop to put shoes on, but right now I'm not really thinking about shoes.

I sit down in the wet grass, and it sends chills up and down my spine. I'm already shivering, but now I think I might be sick.

Then Brian pops into my head, and even though I haven't been opening up to him about anything, seeing his face in my mind makes me feel like I want to talk. Not right now, in the freezing-cold grass, but soon, at our next session.

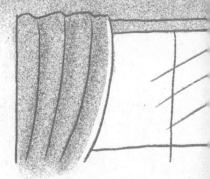

Ding-donnnnng.

My eyes open and I'm on the couch in the living room. I thought I heard the doorbell.

Ding-donnnnng.

I did hear the doorbell. I normally let someone else see who it is, but someone else isn't coming so I guess I have to do it myself.

After last night's freeze-a-thon, I'm a little slow getting up, but I do, and drag myself to the front door.

"Hey!"

It's Theo, with all his hockey equipment.

"We're gonna play street hockey."

I rub my eyes.

"I just got up."

"Well, that means you're ready to play! See you in a couple minutes."

He runs off toward the cul-de-sac.

I do love street hockey, but I'm not much of an athlete, and when I say "not much" I mean "not at all."

I run upstairs anyway, throw some warm clothes on, and then head back down to the garage to grab my stick and ball.

When I finally get down there, I see the other kids from the neighborhood—Brooke, Cole, Gavin, Blake, Nathan, Emily, and of course Theo.

If you're wondering why we invite girls to play, it's because these girls can PLAY. Brooke has one of the best slap shots in our neighborhood, and Emily can run circles around us when she gets going.

"Okay," Theo says. "Let's go. Brooke and Emily, you pick teams."

Brooke goes first.

"Theo."

Emily pauses for a second.

"Ummm. Blake."

Brooke picks quickly.

"Gavin."

"Cole."

"Nathan."

Then Emily looks at me. The only one left.

"That's okay," I say, but I'm not surprised. I'm always the last one picked.

Nathan and Cole face off at center.

I'm back on defense because I'm pretty good at stopping shots.

With the ball between them, Nathan and Cole click their sticks together three times and the game starts. Gavin gets the ball and passes it back to Brooke, who dribbles it up as only she can.

Then Brooke passes it to Theo, who can be really dangerous when he's on a roll. He also likes to talk.

"Here I come, Benny. Get ready to weep."

Theo keeps the ball and dribbles easily past my teammates. I start backing up, waiting for him to get near me so I can hit the ball away with my stick.

He's a good dribbler, but I'm zeroed in on the ball as he shifts it back and forth with his stick.

I start moving forward and shove my stick in front of Theo.

He gets closer and closer.

And at the last second…

The ball goes over my stick and right to Brooke, who slaps it

WHAP!

right into the goal.

"Nice shot, Brooke," Theo yells.

I growl. "You always get me with that!"

"Keep practicing, slowpoke."

And he's right. I don't practice enough, but I really only like playing when everyone else is playing. I don't want to get THAT good. But I do want to stop Theo's stupid flick shot.

Emily takes the ball for our team and checks it in, then passes the ball to me. I'm okay at dribbling, but luckily, Cole is better, so I pass the ball to him.

"Nice pass, Benny!" Cole yells.

He sees Emily open in the corner and passes it to her, but Theo puts his stick in the way and steals it.

I shift gears and start backtracking and trying to get in position to block Theo, but he's coming at me like a runaway train, dribbling left and right.

I'm NOT going to let him get by me.

No way.

Not this time.

And the closer Theo gets, the more my heart starts racing and the more focused I get. I've got to stop him and I reach out with my stick to block the shot and...

He runs past me and scores.

"GRRRRRRR!" I scream.

"It's okay, Ben," Brooke yells.

"Yeah, Ben! It's just a game," Theo says.

Now I'm annoyed and we keep playing and I keep trying to remember it's just a game but I can't. Theo keeps flicking and flicking the ball over my stick and at some point I can't take it anymore and

I throw my stick into the air like a boomerang, but it doesn't come back to me. It flies into one of the side yards and gets stuck in a tree.

"Geez, Ben. Calm down," Theo says. "Seriously."

I stand there breathing heavy with all the other kids staring at me. I don't like the way I feel and don't know what to say or do, so I turn around and storm off to the house, forgetting about my stick in the tree.

"Come back, Ben!" Theo shouts, but I ignore him and all the others who are yelling for me to come back and play.

The more I try, the worse it gets. That should be my motto.

So I just lie on my bed with my face in my pillow, which is where I find myself a lot these days.

"What's wrong, Benny?" Libby asks from the door.

"Nothing. Just go away."

"Here, take this."

I can't resist looking at what Libby is holding in her hand.

She walks toward my bed and opens her hand. It's a Tootsie Roll. It's kind of warm from being in her hand, but I open it and pop it into my mouth.

"Thanks," I say as I immediately start chewing it.

And for a minute, it's just Libby and me sitting on my bed eating Tootsie Rolls, and nothing else matters.

Well, one thing matters.

"Can I have another piece?"

"Sure."

We head into her room to check out her candy collection.

"You can have these."

Smarties. I love Smarties. I like to unwrap the tube, then pour the whole stack into my mouth all at once. There's so much sugar in them that it hurts my teeth, but it's worth it.

Spending time with Libby gives me a little sense of what it's like to be her and how she's dealing with everything.

She just pretends that there's nothing else going on except the thing she is doing at that exact moment. She's only eight but has already figured out how to handle things.

I have a different kind of brain. Once ideas get in there, I can't get them out. They just stay in there and bounce and rattle around.

I try to draw them out, sleep them off, and drown them in the bathtub, but they always bubble up.

I think I'm cursed.

Dad had to leave us alone for a while so he could go to his cancer treatment. I say bye to Libby and head downstairs.

I stop and stare out the front window toward the cul-de-sac and wonder if I should go back and play, even though I walked away from my best friend and all the other kids and acted like a baby. I should at least go and get my stick and ball.

But then I look toward the front porch and see something.

I know for sure it was Theo who brought them to me. He rescued my only stick from high in a tree, and that makes me smile.

My dad pulls into the driveway and I wonder how his treatment went.

He slowly gets out of the car like he's in pain and shuffles to the house, carrying a small bag of groceries.

JAKE!

"Hey there. Are Jake and Libby inside?"
"Libby's here. I haven't seen Jake," I say.
I hear Jake's bedroom door open.
"What."

"Come down here, please. You too, Libby."

He sounds a little out of breath.

Jake barrels down the stairs, takes off from the last step, and lands with a...THUD! The whole house shakes.

"Stop doing that, please," Dad says.

Jake just laughs.

"Your mom called and wants you to stay over next weekend."

That's a surprise. We haven't been to her house yet and she left five months ago.

"She said she's finally ready to take you for the weekend."

Take us for the weekend? That makes it sound like she's pet-sitting.

"Oh, and could you guys put this away where it belongs?"

He hands Jake the grocery bag.

"Do it soon. There's raw meat in there."

Dad slowly makes his way up the stairs as Jake, Libby, and I take the grocery bag to the kitchen. Jake takes out the meat from the bag and smells it.

sniff
sniff

While he pokes at it, Libby and I put everything else away. Cereal, yogurt. Toothpaste. Cigarettes.

Dad normally keeps all his cigarettes in his pocket, so I don't know where the pack needs to go. I hold it up for Libby and Jake to see and without speaking, we agree on the exact place.

I stuff it deep down into the kitchen trash, where Dad will never find it. Then we all look at one another and smile, and for the first time in a really long time I feel like we're all related again, not just three forgotten kids who happen to live under the same roof.

And that makes me happy.
I think that makes us all happy.

9

I told Brian I would keep coming to my appointments but when I get here, I just sit and stare out the window. It's been like this the last few times. I haven't run out again, which I guess is a good thing, but we don't talk about much either.

It's just that every time I have a thought I want to talk about, I freeze up. Like right now.

"How're you feeling today, Benny?"

I shrug.

Brian wiggles his pen between his fingers and taps it twice against his notepad.

"I told you that you were in control and that's still the deal, but I'll say this—the best way that we can get something out of these sessions is for you to pick a topic to start with. It can be anything."

Anything?

"You could start by talking about something that's good in your life. What's good these days?"

I shrug again.

"I can see in your eyes that you have some positive things to share."

I look up at him and wonder how he sees that. I haven't even said anything.

"Your eyes get a little twinkle when you think about things you enjoy."

I shut my eyes to stop the twinkling.

The more I sit here, the less I want to talk to Brian. I thought I wanted to, but now I don't. It's like my mouth is glued shut and to get anything out of it you'd have to pry it open with a screwdriver.

"Okay. Let's switch gears," Brian says. He reaches behind his chair and pulls out a bag. He brings out a spiral-bound sketchbook and a couple of pencils, already sharpened. He presents them to me like a magician would.

"I hear you're a pretty good artist."

I take them from him and nod.

"Drawing your thoughts might help you talk about them."

I put the sketchbook on my lap and open it. The first page is as white as a snowstorm, but I'm drawn to it. Drawing is something I love, and I'm really good at it.

So I start drawing.

This line...then that line...a circle here and another circle inside of it. The room is silent, except for the scratching of my pencil as I add some shading.

It only takes a couple of minutes and I do a pretty good job, even though I'm not used to someone watching me draw.

"May I see it?" asks Brian.

I hold up the drawing.

"You ARE good! That looks like a real eye."

I smile and put the sketchbook in my lap.

"Can you draw the other eye?"

"Yeah, I guess so."

I start drawing the other eye, but it's hard because I have to make sure the pupil's not in the wrong spot or they'll look cross-eyed. It's tricky to get it just right.

And suddenly...out of the blue...without warning...I have an urge to speak. It's like a thought dripped into my mouth and I have to spit it out.

Brian waits to respond, but I see his eyes widen.

"Oh my. I'm so sorry, Ben."

"Yeah." I keep shading the other eye, but I notice that it's way off, so I erase part of it and start again.

"He threw a lasagna pan against the wall the other night."

"That doesn't sound good. Things must be very hard for your family."

"Yeah, I guess so."

If we were a family, it would be hard. But it's not like we talk about it. We don't talk about anything.

And all of a sudden I don't want to talk anymore either. And the eye I redrew looks bad so I erase it. All of it.

I shut the sketchbook and my mouth, too.

"You look sad now, Ben."

I look back at him.

"Your eyes get a little glassy when you think of something sad."

I can't move and can't run out and I'm sort of stuck here staring at Brian. My eyes start to tingle and my bottom lip starts to puff up and the drip that came from my brain earlier is starting again, but this time it's not coming out of my mouth, it's coming out of my eyes.

I try hard not to cry. I feel the drips building up like a stream near a beaver dam and tears start to roll down my cheeks.

Brian hands me the box of tissues.

"What are you feeling, Ben?"

I miss my mom and I miss my dad and all the thoughts I have are in one big pile in my head and I don't know which one to focus on and it's just a big lump and why am I here, and finally, out of frustration, I squish my eyes together.

"I HATE THIS!!!"

"Why do you hate this, Ben?"

"I just do. I hate coming here and I hate drawing and I hate you."

"Well, those are some strong feelings."

He sits back in his chair.

"How do your sister and brother feel about all that's happening?"

"I don't care."

"If you feel like you trust them, which I'm sure you do, how about trying to talk to them about everything that's going on?"

I'm breathing heavy and looking at Brian, who I thought was really smart but not anymore after that stupid idea.

Dad picks me up on time, and as soon as I get in the car, I'm smothered by the smell of smoke.

We drive off and I stare out the window. A thought drips into my mouth and I spit it out.

Dad breathes out his nose, which means that he's annoyed.

"Oh, now YOU'RE going to get on my case?"

He takes one last puff, then flicks the cigarette out the window.

Then he breathes out his nose again because he's mad. He turns the radio up loud and we don't say anything else the whole way home.

When we get there I go to my room and shut the door. My backpack is on my desk. I haven't unzipped it in over a week. That's not a good thing, because I know for a fact that there are some tests coming up and I'm behind on my homework.

I lie on the bed and think about going to my mom's this weekend and about Brian's dumb idea about trying to talk with Libby and Jake. If I did talk to them, where would I start?

I hear pounding coming from Dad's room.

BANG!
BANG!
BANG!

I run and stand outside his door.

"Dad, are you okay?"

"Yeah, Benny. I'm fine."

I crack the door to look inside and expect my dad to yell at me to go away, but he's lying on the bed and rubbing his fist.

It's dark in his room because he has all the blinds drawn, and he doesn't look happy. I walk over to where he's lying and stop right in front of him. It looks like he's been crying and it scares me a little because I've never seen him cry.

He looks up at me, then reaches out his hand for me to grab it, and I do. He pulls me close to him and gives me a giant bear hug.

It's weird and I sort of want to pull away but I don't.

Luckily, he lets me go because he was kind of choking me a little.

He rolls onto his back and lets out a big sigh. I don't know what to say to him and maybe I don't need to say anything. So I just lean down and give him another hug. Then I kiss him on the forehead. He's kind of sweaty and when I lean back up, I have to wipe my face.

He opens one eye like a vampire waking from a deep sleep.

But he's smiling, which is a good thing, and I smile back. Then he closes his eyes again.

I hear someone walking up the stairs and by the sound of the giant King Kong footsteps, I know it's Jake.

Then I hear a door shut.

So I leave my dad's room, closing his door behind me, and walk down the hall to Libby's.

Knock, knock.

No answer. I peek inside, just to make sure she's not hiding.

Nope. She's gone.

Jake is in his room because I can hear him drumming. At least that's what it sounds like.

Knock, knock.

He doesn't answer.

I knock louder.

Nothing.

I slowly open the door and see him sitting in a chair, drumming on the desk with his hands. He has headphones on and is really getting into it.

He sees me and tosses off his headphones.

"What do you want?"

"Nothing. Just seeing what you're doing."

"Well, next time you better knock."

"I knocked twice."

"Oh...well, then next time don't knock at all. Which means, don't bother me."

I look at his stereo.

"What are you listening to?"

"Nothing you would like."

I pick up the album cover.

He's right. I wouldn't like it.

"You sure have a lot of cologne."

I pick up the one called Really Manly and he grabs it out of my hand.

"By the way, have you been using my deodorant?"

I pause for a second. "No."

"Are you sure?" He takes the cap off his sport stick. "Because it's really smooth on top and as you can see..."

He lifts his sleeve up.

"My pits aren't smooth at all."

Backstory: My brother matured very early. I think he had armpit hair when he was still in diapers.

He's only thirteen and his chest has a goatee.

"The only way that my deodorant could be smooth on the top is if someone with smooth armpits used it."

He grabs my arm and lifts it up, then pulls my sleeve down.

"Stop using my deodorant, Skin Pits."

I pull my arm away and run off.

"Skin Pits? Ha ha ha ha ha," I hear him say, and he keeps laughing.

I slam the door behind me. So much for family bonding.

10

The first car ride to Mom's new house is dead silent, if you don't count the thumping windshield wipers and the wet road below us. Dad has the window cracked like he always does, to let his cigarette smoke blow out. It never works and isn't working now.

Jake is messing with the radio, trying to find a good rock station. He just flips and flips until finally Dad smacks his hand, then turns the knob himself until he locates his country station.

The rain is spitting down and the wipers are thumping and Dad is singing out loud and tapping his college ring on the steering wheel as we make our way to Mom's.

It takes a little while to get there, as we drive by houses and buildings that I've never seen before. Dad turns this way, then drives, then turns that way. I have no idea what part of town Mom lives in, or even if it's in the same town. But it seems far away, and I feel like I've been in the car too long. When we finally pull up to where Mom lives, I jump right out.

The rain isn't as bad outside as it sounded inside the car. It's still drizzling a little bit, enough to make my hair wet, but I don't have to run for cover or anything.

I look over at Dad, who's standing outside his car door, finishing his cigarette. Then I scan the row of houses and try to figure out which one is Mom's. They all sort of look the same. Some have decorations on the front door, some have bare windows, and some have curtains. One even has an awning.

"It's that one," Dad shouts. "Number 201." My eyes stop on the number. Mom's house is the one with the curtains in the window, and it's a little run-down on the outside with peeling paint, rusty railings, and a broken gutter.

In fact, as I look around I notice the whole neighborhood is kind of the same way.

Jake leads and Libby follows, but not before jumping in a big puddle. I take one step, then turn around to wait for Dad.

Our eyes meet, and after a few seconds, it's clear he's not coming with us to the front door and I get a little nervous. Then he winks and gets in the car.

The rain picks up and so does my heartbeat—*thump, thump, thump.* As my head gets wetter, raindrops start rolling down my face. I lower my head and turn toward the house.

That's when I see a worm. He's floating dead in the puddle that Libby jumped in.

I wonder if he was already dead and shriveled up before the rain, or if the rain actually drowned him.

Jake rings the doorbell.

There's silence for a few seconds, but then you can hear Mom's voice getting louder and louder and she comes to open the door.

It opens with a long squeak.

Mom greets us with a happy tone in her voice that sounds phony. She makes it seem as if there was no divorce and nothing out of the ordinary has ever happened to our family. She is really good at acting.

She holds the door open and checks us all out as we file through the entry, making sure that Dad is doing a good job of feeding us and dressing us and everything else that a good parent should do.

I look back at Dad but he already drove off.

"Hey, Benny, you look like you gained some weight," she says, and pats me on the stomach. There's really not anything you can say to a comment like that, so I look her in the eyes and stay quiet, even as she gives me a hug. I hug her back, but not hard.

Mom lets go of me and as soon as she does, I look down.

Next to the front door is a plant in a Mexican pot that she bought on one of her trips a few years ago.

It's a cool pot with orange and gold designs hand-painted on it. It was even cooler when it was at our house.

Now it's here. And now it's ugly.

The plant is dead, too.

We pile inside Mom's house.

"So, whaddya think?" she asks.

There's a bookshelf in one corner and the books look really familiar. It's not like I ever read any of them, but they're all books that used to be at our house. That chair over there, too. That's ours. The couch? Ours. And the framed picture of a flower bouquet and the clock on the wall that has never worked since I've been alive. It's all ours.

It's like my mom snuck in one day and stole everything out of our house. And it just feels wrong.

Libby would say something like that.

My breathing gets faster and my eyebrows tense up and my eyes squish together. All this time I thought I wanted to see my mom, but now I don't want to see her at all.

I'm stuck here for the weekend, so I turn on the TV and just stare at it, not wanting to do or say anything.

I sit there while Jake plays records and Libby helps Mom with dinner in the kitchen.

After a few minutes, I get bored and wander into the kitchen to see what they're making, but I don't say anything to either of them. I'm still too upset.

At bedtime, it becomes clear that Jake and I don't have beds to sleep in. Mom's plan is that

Princess Libby is going to sleep with her in the cushy queen bed and Peasants Jake and Benny are going to sleep on the office floor in sleeping bags. But there's just one problem.

"You don't have sleeping bags?"

"Dad didn't say we needed them," Jake says.

Mom sighs and shakes her head.

"Your father...never thinking ahead."

For as long as it took for us to get invited to Mom's house, you'd think she would have thought ahead, too, and made a nice space for us to sleep.

I look into the office and it barely has furniture. It's filled with stacks and stacks of boxes.

Even if we did have sleeping bags, I'm not sure where they would go.

When we finally push some boxes aside and clear two areas to sleep, Mom gives us a bunch of tiny blankets to lay down for padding, and we set up our little sleeping areas. She gives us pillows, of course, but they're really hard, like I'm laying my head on someone's leg. Jake and I finally get settled and turn out the light, and right away, the room feels cold and echoey.

I hear Mom's and Libby's muffled voices from the other room, mixed with the slow, rumbling thunder from outside.

The night sounds seem to get louder and louder and the air in the room seems to get colder and colder. As we lie there I start to get scared. I squish my eyes tight trying to block everything out. My blood starts racing and swishing through my veins—*thump, thump, thump*—and I try with all my might to stay calm.

And out of nowhere...

I think of clouds. They're big and white and fluffy and I'm flying through them, up and down, in and out, far away from here. I fly past eagles and airplanes and blimps and then a random balloon passes by. I fly for what seems like hours. I swoop here and swoop there and do loop-de-loops with the ocean glittering below. And in my mind, I start swooping down to earth, faster and faster until I see the ground coming at me really fast, but then, at the last second, I pull my body and swoop up, then make a soft landing. My eyes stop squishing so much, my breathing comes back to normal, and the thumping of my heartbeat stops.

I lie there staring at the ceiling and sweating a little bit, wondering if I will ever get to sleep.

Then Jake reaches over to me.

I look at him and wonder if he's joking or not because he's never wondered how I'm doing before. For the first time in a long time, this feels real. I mean, we had a bonding moment over hiding Dad's cigarettes, but this is different.

I think he actually cares.

"Yeah, I'm okay," I answer.

And we lie there, not saying much.

I really want to go to sleep, but Jake has other ideas.

"These are some really nice beds, huh?"

And I laugh, but don't say anything back because all I want to do is go to sleep.

Jake does an imitation of crickets.

CHIRP... CHIRP... CHIRP...

I laugh at that, too, but I don't want to.

"Stop! I'm trying to sleep!"

"Okay, Ben. You can go to sleep."

And I think I'm going to sleep.

Then Jake starts making funny spit sounds with his mouth and laughing and it's not funny but it's totally funny and I can't help but crack up along with him.

The more we laugh, the calmer I get, and the dark doesn't seem so dark, and the blankets don't seem so tiny, and my pillow doesn't feel like a leg, and I stop thinking about Mom stealing our stuff.

Strangely, as annoying as Jake can be, and I can't believe I'm saying this—my older brother feels like my hero.

We talk about missing home and wonder if Dad ever found his cigarettes but then we get back to cracking jokes and doing fart noises and burping the alphabet and forgetting that we're both lying on a cold wooden office floor with tiny blankets and tons of boxes all around us.

11

School just isn't my thing. Maybe it was once, but not lately.

Studying is hard.

Pop quizzes are hard.

And doing homework? Borrr-innggg.

There are so many other things that I'd rather be doing.

Drawing.

Watching TV.

Being outside.

If there wasn't any work to do, school would be okay because I'd get to talk with my friends and have recess and draw on the chalkboard.

Mrs. Lord is one of my teachers and she's really nice. She's my homeroom teacher, and she teaches us English and math and a lot of times we watch presentations and films on the

pull-down screen. If it were up to her, she'd probably let us draw on the chalkboard all day if we wanted.

Then there's my other teacher, Mr. Rodgers. He is the total opposite of nice. He teaches us social studies and science and does it with a grumpy look on his face. He talks really loud and isn't very patient with anyone. Rumor has it that he pushed a kid up against the wall once, but I don't know if that's true. Maybe he didn't because he still has a job, but maybe he did.

Even so, he's just…so…boring.

Sitting in his class and listening to him ramble on about presidents and the Bill of Rights or even photosynthesis puts me to sleep. A deep sleep. Like a coma.

Here's how he sounds:

He just goes on and on.

For the record, Rutherford B. Hayes was the nineteenth president of the United States. I did a book report on him.

Right now, my textbook is looking mighty empty along the margins.

So I start filling it in.

I start out with an eye, but it slowly turns into a portrait of my least-favorite social studies and science teacher ever.

I give it Mr. Rodgers's overgrown eyebrows, big nose, comb-over hair, and, of course, his chin that looks like a tiny butt. Then I draw his patented grumpy frown and add a skinny neck with an over-size collar and an ugly tie. It's a masterpiece.

But it does need something else.

Hmmm.

The perfect headline...

Ha. Got it.

"Mr. Brooks?" says Mr. Rodgers.

I look up, surprised that he called on me.

"What was the first colony in the United States?"

"Umm." I know the answer to this, but because he surprised me, it's on the tip of my tongue and I can't spit it out.

"Do you have something you want to show me?" He starts walking down the aisle toward my desk.

I look down at the drawing, then close my book in a panic.

"Or maybe you want to share it with the class?"

"No," I say, leaning on top of my textbook.

He stops at my desk and hovers over it like a vulture.

"Would you please hand me your book?"

I'm cornered and I don't know what to do and there isn't a way out and I wish I didn't know how to draw because this wouldn't have happened.

Mr. Rodgers grabs the book and pulls it out from under my arms.

He flips through it, page after page, adding suspense to the situation with every page he turns.

Finally, he comes to my drawing.

"Hmmm. Look, class."

He holds up the book and shows it around the room. "Mr. Brooks thinks I'm a jerk. How delightful."

Everyone laughs. He looks down at me.

"Now, Mr. Brooks, why am I a jerk?"

I shrug.

"Is it (a), because I'm teaching you things you don't want to learn about?"

I don't answer. But yes, that is true.

"Is it (b), because I'm mean and horrible and don't care about my students?"

That might be true, but I stay silent.

"Or is it (c), because students draw offensive pictures in costly textbooks and ruin school property so I have to send them to the office?"

Letter c. Definitely letter c.

He walks to his desk and pulls out a blank hall pass. He fills it out really fast and signs it with an overdramatic flair.

"Please take all of your things with you to the office. They will make arrangements to have your parents pick you up. Goodbye, Mr. Brooks."

He holds out the hall pass.

If you've ever drawn in a textbook, then gotten in trouble for it, then had to gather your stuff and make the shame-faced walk from your desk to the principal's office, you know how horribly embarrassing it can be.

Even though Theo and Gavin are looking at me and laughing to themselves, it's not really that funny and just makes things worse for me. I'm the one who has to get kicked out of class and sit outside the principal's office and then have my dad come pick me up.

I wonder if I'm going to get the paddle. Legend has it that Dr. Goodhart, our school principal, has an electric paddle hidden in his office.

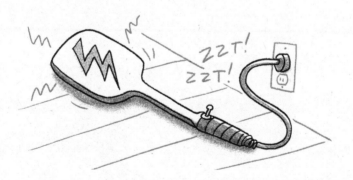

When bad kids come in, he quietly closes the door and takes out the electric paddle and whaps kids' butts and he just keeps on whapping until the kids' butts are totally destroyed.

I've never seen it and I don't know anyone who has. I hope today isn't the day.

After a while, I notice my dad walk into the school lobby, then through the office doors, and he looks like he's so tired he's about to fall over. I know he's got cancer and everything, but I kind of wish he does fall over before he gets to me. Then he can't wring my neck for getting kicked out of class.

He looks at me with evil eyes as he breathes a sigh of frustration. Then he turns to the receptionist and signs me out for the rest of the day.

The car ride home is quiet. Really quiet. Quieter than it is when I'm in the tub and I put my head underwater. And no fart-bubble sounds.

I just sit there.

"Are you that bored at school?"

"Yes. School is boring. Especially Mr. Rodgers's class."

"You gotta knock that stuff off and get serious. No more of this!"

THIS. Yeah, this. THIS is what it looks like when a family falls apart and there's nothing to look forward to every day when I get home. THIS is what it looks like when your dad is grumpy and has cancer and is trying to get better but isn't because the thing that caused the cancer is still happening. THIS is my life. THIS. THIS.

"What?!"

"Yep, and this time, it's a full month. No going out. No friends. No drawing. No nothing."

This sounds really bad for me, which it should be, but I'm not worried. My dad has a way of laying down the law and following it strictly for about one day. On the second day, he barely remembers it happening, and by the third day, it's like I was never grounded in the first place. I'll be going to Theo's and watching TV and drawing in no time at all and nothing else will ever be said.

LA LA LAAAAA!

For the next twenty-four hours I stay inside. Day 2 arrives and I start drawing, and I start calling Theo, and at some point on Day 3, I just leave the house altogether, knowing that I'm in the clear.

This kind of stuff happened when my dad DIDN'T have cancer, but now it's sort of like we don't have parents at all.

Now that I'm back to real life and homework and tests and taking out the trash and setting silverware and stuff, I start thinking of getting away.

The bike. I really want one. Riding Theo's was amazing, but having one of my own would mean I could jump on it anytime and ride as fast and as far away as I want to. The problem is that Dad never remembers to give us our allowance, so I can't save up. He gets mad if we ask for it, so I'm kind of stuck. Luckily, Christmas is around the corner.

So I give it one more shot.

Dad, I really want a bike for Christmas.

"Benny, we've talked about this, and geez, you just won't let up."

"But Dad..."

"And tell me why you should have a bike with your attitude the way it is and getting in trouble at school and drawing your teacher's face in your textbook."

I've got to hand it to him—he's right.

I don't deserve it.

But I want it.

And thinking about wanting it and not getting it makes my eyes squish together and my stomach turn, and when I try to think about being better and don't know how to get better, it gets worse. And I'm mad. I'm really mad.

And that means I won't be able to sleep and when I can't sleep, the dark seems darker, and the air seems colder, and I lie awake staring at the ceiling and, well, you know the rest.

I hear my dad coughing and it won't stop and things just keep getting worse and I wonder if I'll ever get to fly in those clouds or if I'm just nailed down to this stupid life of mine forever.

12

"It's pretty slim this year, guys."

Dad sits back in his pajamas and lights up a Christmas-morning cigarette.

With each little gift I open—a Magic 8 Ball, a pack of bubble gum—I can't help thinking there's a bigger gift hidden somewhere in the room. The one with handlebars. And wheels. And pedals.

Another pair of socks—like I need those. Colored underwear? White works just fine.

My eyes dart around the room expecting to catch a glimpse of it in the corner, or behind the couch, or way back behind the Christmas tree. Maybe Dad will slip out of here in a second, go to the garage, and act all surprised when he brings in the big gift.

Not to be greedy, but the bike is really all I want. Forget about the useful socks and underwear, the delicious candy and fun games. The bike—it's the number one thing on my mind, with nothing else coming even close. I think it might be the single most amazing gift I could ever get. Libby and Jake got some cool stuff. Jake has been wanting an electronic football game and Libby, of course, got more stuffed animals.

We all chipped in and got Dad a figurine at the drugstore that says *Dad of the Year*.

"Thanks, guys!" he says half-heartedly. I'm not sure if he actually liked the gift or not, but he acts like he did, then he puts the gift on the floor next to the chair.

But back to my big gift—I haven't seen Dad get up, and the corners of the room are empty, and the idea of getting a bike for Christmas is slipping away.

Ooh. But wait...

We're going to Mom's in a few hours. There's still hope! Finally! I see the benefit of having two houses. Double the presents and the chance for a GRAND PRIZE!!!

Dad stands up, looks like he's about to fall over from exhaustion, then sits back down.

"We'll do it, Daddy," Libby says, and my dad sinks into the chair and closes his eyes.

Later, we get to Mom's and the thought that my bike might be here, waiting for me in all its glory, has got me excited. As we gather together in the living room to open gifts, I'm on the edge of my seat trying to stay calm.

Mom makes an announcement. "Okay, every-body has their own little pile to open."

"Little"? That's not what I want to hear. Little is not good.

Libby opens one gift first.

"Oooh, a coat! I need one."

She's right. Her winter coat has smudges and dirt all over it, plus her arms have gotten longer and stick out of the sleeves.

Jake opens one next.

It's an album of some band.

"You'll know their song," Mom says. "It's on the radio."

"Sing it," Jake says.

"I don't know exactly how it goes. But once you listen, you'll remember it."

Jake is looking at the record like it is a mystery he doesn't feel like solving.

Then Mom hands me one of my gifts.

Obviously, it is NOT a bike, but I try to act excited anyway. I take the bow off gently. Mom actually makes some really nice bows. She takes regular ribbon and ties the box shut, then uses the end of the scissors and scrapes along the ribbon so that it curls up.

I pull off the wrapping paper and see an old shoebox.

Hmm. I wonder what could be inside.

I take off the lid…

and pull back the tissue paper…

It's a stuffed raccoon, the kind that you would get if you were two years old, with big plastic eyes and a half smile so cute you would hug it and squeeze it all day and take it with you in the stroller and have it sit next to you in your high chair and fall asleep with it at bedtime. IF YOU WERE TWO!

I look up at Mom with a "what the heck" look.

"Your father said you've been having trouble sleeping. I thought he could keep you company."

She does know I'm ten now, right?

"How is counseling going?"

She's asking me about my counseling as I hold a stuffed raccoon. Kind of embarrassing. So I don't answer.

We open the rest of our gifts.

One after the other.

And one after the other, my bike doesn't appear. I call it MY bike, but it's not even close to being mine yet. And it looks like it won't be this year, either, and honestly, maybe not ever.

And that's our Christmas.

It would be fun with more people and more presents, but Mom doesn't keep in touch with her relatives. She had a really bad childhood and doesn't like to talk about her side of the family.

Dad doesn't talk to his family either. According to Mom, he's burned a lot of bridges with bad decisions, lying, and other things that I'm probably too young to know about.

My point for talking about all of this is to say that our Christmases are pretty lousy. It's just us, which I guess is okay because we don't have to get in the car and go spend the day at a relative's house like a lot of the other kids I know do. But it's still lonely.

Mom heads off to the kitchen to whip up Christmas dinner. The oven has been on all afternoon, and the kitchen is hot, and the whole house smells like food.

At some point we sit down to eat at the tiny table, where there is not much room for anything, but it's okay because I'm starving.

When someone has to ask for a compliment, it makes the compliment kind of hard to give. Mom does that all the time, but today, to keep things simple, all I say to her is "Yes, Mom." But I really don't think this is the best gravy I've ever had. Sometimes when I eat at school, the cafeteria gravy is really good. Maybe even the best, if I'm being honest.

Mom's mashed potatoes are good. The stuffing, too. This meal is pretty much the same meal we eat at Thanksgiving. Mom and Dad both make their turkey really, really dry.

DONK! DONK!

The dark meat is okay, but the rest of it? Yuck.

"That turkey is so good. Isn't it good?"

No, Mom. It's not.

Jake mumbles "Mm-hmm" under his breath, without looking up. I told you he eats anything.

And with a last swallow of food and some dish cleaning, Christmas comes to an end. No fanfare or fireworks, just sore teeth from chewing on that turkey.

I head up to Mom's office. I can't stop thinking about my bike. It's a really easy thing to buy. You can get them anywhere. I could be riding it right now instead of dragging myself up the stairs.

An hour or so later, Jake is still wandering around downstairs, watching TV or something. Then I hear the fridge open and Mom yells,

PUT THE FOOD AWAY!

She shouts again from her bedroom: "Guys, I work tomorrow. Very early. I'll be back around lunchtime."

I lie there and look at the ceiling. I want my mom not to work on the weekends that we're here and I want to have an actual bed when I come visit and not this dumb blanket pad.

My eyes are like saucers, big and round with no thoughts about falling asleep.

But other thoughts start trickling in. The darkness. The bike. The floor.

Gifts. Christmas. Dad. Cancer. Turkey. Cancer. Underwear. Sand. Cancer cancer cancer.

And before I know it, my mind is thinking about everything all at once and I can't stop it, and finally it's just one big glob of thoughts packed into my little skull.

I roll over to my left and my arm hits something soft.

The stuffed raccoon is lying next to me on the floor. I'm not sure how he got here, because I didn't bring him upstairs, but his fur feels soft on my hand.

I grab him and pull him to my chest.

I look him in the eyes, but it's so dark I can't really see him.

But I can feel him. He's got two short ears and two smooth shiny eyes and when I run my fingers across his face I can feel his little smile. I turn him to the side and see the silhouette of his long, fuzzy, ringed tail in the back light of the window.

I pull him close to me again and think it would be a good idea to give him a name.

The Stuffed Raccoon is a horrible name.

How about Rocky? Nah.

Raccoony? Stupid.

Milton? Too random.

He needs a better name.

Not that it has to be a boy's name, either.

Tracy? Stella? It just doesn't fit.

So I keep thinking.

Sam? Buster?

This may take a while. For now, his name will have to be Stuffed Raccoon.

I turn over and stare into the dark with Stuffed Raccoon pulled tight against my chest, and Jake still downstairs messing around.

✧ ✧ ✧

Early the next morning, I hear Mom's footsteps from the next room as she walks around getting ready for work. When I finally wake all the way up, she's gone.

The sun is shining through the blinds so I throw my arms over my eyes like a vampire would.

The house is quiet and I look to see if Jake is sleeping.

He's not there.

The blankets look just like they did when I went to sleep last night.

I go downstairs to find him. He's not in the bathroom, not on the front porch, not anywhere. I run back upstairs to see if he's being sneaky and hiding out in a closet or the corner of Mom's room.

Nope.

But then I think maybe he's hiding behind a door and waiting to jump out and scare me like he always does.

So I check behind all the doors. Even the hall closet.

He doesn't pop out, but I wish he would.

"Where's Jake?" I ask Libby, who is just half-awake and flipping her pillow to the cool side.

"I don't know," she mumbles.

This is not good. Maybe even really bad. I look all around the house again, in every nook and cranny.

I'm getting really nervous now, so I call my dad. I call him because his is the only phone number I know by heart. Except Theo's. But I have trouble remembering that sometimes.

Briiinnng!

He doesn't answer.

Briiinnng!

He still doesn't pick up.

My stomach starts to churn waiting for Dad to answer, but ring after ring, he doesn't.

I hang up and stare at the floor, not knowing what to do next.

Then I think of my mom leaving and my dad not around and now my brother is gone and I'm here all alone and how any other time in my life I want Jake gone but now, right now, I would love for him to be home.

And to add to it all, I'm at my mom's...so I can't call my mom!

I pace around the kitchen in my socks, slipping and sliding with each step. Then I sit down at

Mom's tiny kitchen table, squish my eyes together, and think.

But nothing comes.

Drip drip drip.

The faucet in Mom's kitchen catches my attention, so I look up.

And that's when I see it.

A piece of paper sitting on the counter next to the stove.

I'm at work
555-2755
Ⓜ

13

"He's gone?" yells Mom. "Whaddya mean, he's gone?"

"He's just gone. I looked all over for him."

She breathes out heavily.

"Okay. I'll be home in a few minutes. Stay there!"

It doesn't take fifteen minutes for Mom to burst through the front door.

"Jake!!!" Mom growls in anger even though Jake isn't here.

The police are just thirty seconds behind her, which means she must have called them before she left work.

Woooooop wooooooo goes the siren.

From inside the house, it looks like a mini manhunt. Mom and three police officers, two men and a woman, gather next to the street, pointing this way and nodding, then pointing that way.

Two of the officers get in their car and drive off. Mom stays back with the other one and nods as the officer takes notes.

Libby comes downstairs.

"What happened?" she asks as she rubs her eyes.

"Jake is gone."

"Really? I saw him leave this morning. He had his coat on and everything."

"Where'd he go?"

"I don't know. He just walked by Mom's room."

About an hour passes. Mom's still mad, but the police figure out a way to get her to calm down.

She sits on the couch and blows warm air into her hands.

"Mom?"

"Not now, Ben."

"But…"

Before I can finish, a police car arrives outside with its siren on and Mom jumps up off the couch.

I run to the window and see one of the officers walking around to the side of the car and opening the door.

Out pops Jake, and the officer accompanies him down the sidewalk and to the house. They don't get halfway to the stairs before Mom sprints out the door and starts yelling at Jake, but in a worried kind of way.

"Where did you go?!" And she hugs him really hard like his eyes are going to burst out of his head.

He tries pushing her away as she squeezes harder.

"I'm fine," I hear him mumble. I walk over and watch from the screen door.

"Son, next time, tell your parents where you're headed," says the officer. "That would save everyone a lot of worry. Plus, it's dangerous to walk off at your age, especially in this neighborhood."

Jake nods.

"Thank you, Officers," Mom says with a smile.

"A pleasure, ma'am. And happy holidays."

I step back to let Jake come into the house, and he glances at me. It isn't just a normal glance either.

He has a look in his eyes that someone gives when they just got away with something they shouldn't have. Like when a cartoon cat eats a cartoon mouse. The cat always looks satisfied and at the same time a little menacing.

That's what Jake's look was.

The brilliant part about it is that he got our mom to drop everything in her life to worry and pay attention to him and send the police. I mean, it was a lot of work to pull something like that off, but if you're looking for attention, it was a genius move.

We all gather in the living room, with Jake sitting on the end of the couch, slumped back with his arms crossed.

Mom is lecturing him about scaring her out of her mind, how she had to leave work. She's mad one second, then sad the next, and going back and forth between the two. The whole time Mom is going off on Jake, Libby is clinging to her like a baby koala bear.

Then I look at Jake, then back at Libby, and realize that she's trying to get Mom's attention, too. I mean, we ALL want Mom's and Dad's attention, but it's so hard to come by. But my brother and sister are finding ways to MAKE them pay attention. The whole thing is just really sad.

Back at our real house, I start off the new year by making a deal with myself to try harder in school.

When you're doing bad in school it's easy not to notice until you look at your report card and see how many incompletes you have. And then you look at the teacher's notes about how you need to "pay attention" and "stop daydreaming" and actually "put forth some effort." That makes it pretty clear what needs to change.

The last thing I want to do is flunk fifth grade and be only one grade above Libby next year. How embarrassing would THAT be?

So in math class, I raise my hand and ask questions.

In social studies, even though Mr. Rodgers probably hates my guts, I volunteer to go to the board.

In English, Mrs. Lord asks me to read a passage from our textbook, and I do it, with a smile on my face.

And that's just Monday.

I do that Tuesday...

and Wednesday...

and Thursday...

But by the end of the day Thursday, I'm getting tired of it.

And by Friday, I feel like I'm going to keel over.

It's really hard work to be a good student. I do it for one whole week and it nearly kills me.

whew.

When we get home from school, Mom's car is there again and I dread going inside. Libby and Jake and I look at one another and think back to the last time Mom was here and none of us wanted to go into the house.

So we sit on the porch step.

And sit.

There are no sounds coming from the house and no muffled screams, and no crash of lasagna pans exploding against the wall.

Maybe nobody's home?

Maybe Mom and Dad are having a contest to see who can be the quietest.

Or maybe things are okay. It sounds okay, so it must be okay.

We open the door and head inside. The house is so quiet you could hear a pin drop.

We walk into the living room, through the dining room, and into the kitchen.

Still, no one.

Then I hear Dad's voice coming from the family room and it's deep and quiet. He blows his nose.

We walk into the family room and Dad and Mom are sitting on the couch.

It's weird and confusing to me how two people can fight and hate each other so much one day, then sit together on a couch and be friendly with each other the next.

They're sitting sort of close to each other and it looks like they're good friends. I don't get it.

Dad lets out a long sigh. Then speaks.

"Well, kids." He sighs again.

"The doctor"—he looks at Mom—"the doctor told me today that the cancer is not getting better. In fact, it's growing fast, I—"

My mom butts in.

They told your dad to start preparing for the end.

The end? The end of the day? The week?

The end end? The BIG END?

"He said I would be lucky to make it to the summer."

Well, it's January now.

February.

March.

April.

May.

June.

Five months.

My dad has five months to live.

The thought of my dad having five months to live starts to fill my head like when you have a glass of water and you drop in some food coloring and it slowly takes over the water in the glass.

The more it fills my head, the weaker my legs get.

My knees bend and I can't stop them and I drop to the floor but make it look like I'm doing it on purpose so nobody can tell.

Libby runs to Dad and hugs him. Jake stands and stares into space, speechless. It's hard to turn Jake speechless.

"Come here, guys."

And since I can't walk, I slide on my butt over to the couch, where me, Dad, Mom, Libby, and Jake all form a group hug. And it's like I'm in a dream.

The one wish I've had, the MAIN wish, even more important than a new bike, is that my family all be together, and now we are.

I guess if you're going to wish for anything, you gotta be really specific, because this isn't exactly how I wanted us to be together, bonding over my dad's expiration date.

Dad pats us all on the back, which as everyone knows is the signal for the end of a hug.

Mom looks at Dad.

"I have to go. I'll check back in tomorrow and we'll start making plans."

"Okay," Dad says. Mom stands and stares at him, waiting for him to say something else.

"Thank you," he finally says, and it looks like he means it. But I'm not sure.

Mom hugs Jake, Libby, then me. She squeezes me harder than she usually does, like she is clinging on for her life. That would make sense.

I try standing up, but my legs just aren't strong enough. So I pull myself onto my knees, then swing one leg out. Then with all my strength, I stand up. I look like a baby giraffe, walking for the first time, as my legs wobble with each step.

I make it upstairs and over to Libby's door.

She's stuffing clothes into a backpack, getting ready to go to a sleepover at our neighbor Tara's house.

She zips up her backpack and walks past me out of the room, shutting the door and almost closing my hand in it. Then she heads down the stairs and out the front door.

I open her door, grab a LIFE SAVERS from her desk, then wobble into my room.

I sit on my bed with my head swirling and I picture my dad in a coffin with a cigarette sticking out of his mouth and me repeating fifth grade every year for the rest of my life.

And it's Theo…and Krista…and hockey sticks…
I shove my face into my pillow and scream as hard
as I can for as long as I can until my throat hurts.

14

It's extremely hard going through life looking through a peephole. Right now, I can only really focus on about a twelve-inch space in front of me, and the rest is blurry and gray.

It's even harder trying to play street hockey through a peephole because things go by so fast and you can only focus on something for a split second. When you don't see things, you sort of just start making things up so that it looks like you know what you're doing, but you really don't.

Brooke passes the ball to Cole and Cole passes to me, but I barely touch the ball before Brooke wants the ball back. So I pass it to her. Everything sounds so far away and muffled like I'm listening to it underwater, and at this point I don't really care about even trying to look like I'm into this street hockey game.

But then I'm sort of forced to snap out of my daze. Theo gets the ball and starts dribbling it toward me, with fire in his eyes. If you've ever been daydreaming and then someone snaps you out of it, you know it takes a minute to come back to reality. I grab my stick tight with both hands and bend my knees. I'm going to stop Theo's shot this time. He dribbles in and fakes a pass, and with my head still half-asleep, I put my stick in to block it and—

FLICK!

Right over my stick.

Have you ever heard a teakettle when the water is boiling and it starts to whistle a little bit, then it gets louder and louder until the steam is blowing out so hard it's making the kettle scream and rattle?

Well, that's me right now.

The steam starts in my stomach and builds up through my chest, and then goes into my head and my ears, and out my eyes and ears and

I walk over to Theo and without even hesitating or thinking about it, I push him...hard.

"Hey! Cut it out, Benny!"

"Yeah, Ben, stop being a jerk!" Emily yells.

And quick as I blew my top, I run off straight to my backyard and up a tree.

Halfway, I slip and almost fall because I'm going too fast. I cut my wrist on a broken branch, right in the space between my glove and my coat.

I close my eyes and replay the scene in my mind over and over, and I picture Theo looking at me. I just sit there wondering how this is going to end, and how many people are going to keep dropping out of my life, or how many I'm going to push out.

The bus is extra loud the next afternoon and I'm not in the mood for it. I'm never in the mood for it, and with Theo not talking to me or saving me a seat, it makes it ten times worse. Now it's just me in a seat with the So-and-So brothers, right in front of the person least likely to make my life better—Betsy Morgan.

She's sitting directly behind me and the steady stream of *yaks* coming from her mouth is more than I can take.

It's like there are thirty-seven pinballs in my head and the flappers are going and the balls are hitting bumpers and lights are flashing and popping and she's getting a super-jumbo bonus score.

She yaks and she yaks and her voice seems ultra-loud today until finally I can't stand it anymore and I just turn around and look her in the eyes and say:

WILL YOU
SHUT
UP?!

The front of the bus where we're sitting goes quiet and she looks up at me with a stupid look on her face, then opens her mouth for one final yak.

"Make me!"

Those two words are interesting. Obviously she isn't scared to keep yakking. When someone makes an offer like that to me, it's pretty hard to resist. My arm raises and I tell it to stop and I ponder hitting her and I probably shouldn't but before I can make a real decision about how to handle this...

WHAP!

Betsy looks at me like she's seen a ghost and time stops for what seems like an hour. But then blood starts trickling out of her nose and down her lip. Betsy looks like she's gonna cry. I feel so bad and don't know what to do. Words just won't come out of my mouth.

I'm the first one off at our stop and nobody says bye to me. Jake and Libby are walking behind me.

"You're gonna be in trouble," Jake mumbles. He's probably right, but I try not to think about it.

Betsy must have told her parents because the next day her parents called Principal Goodhart and then Principal Goodhart called my dad, and now I'm sitting slumped on the couch listening to Dad yell at me about how hitting others, especially girls, is unacceptable and how I really need to get ahold of my temper, and how the counseling must not be working and that's okay because it's costing him an arm and a leg anyway.

I just sit there with my head down listening to him ramble on about how to be in control of my feelings.

I feel bad for hitting Betsy, but to get a lecture from Dad on behaving appropriately? It doesn't seem fair.

And right in the middle of it, he starts coughing again. He goes on and on in what might be his biggest coughing fit ever. I sit back on the couch, waiting for it to subside. But it doesn't. He just coughs and coughs and coughs, and I look down and there's blood on the floor. I look up at Dad and his hand is covered with blood and he looks scared. I'm scared, too.

He holds up his hand like he doesn't want me to do anything but just sit here. He runs into the kitchen, still coughing, to grab some paper towels, then calls the doctor. By the way he's talking, he sounds really nervous.

After a few minutes he is calm again and despite what just happened, he still grounds me—this time for two months.

You know how that goes.

Later at counseling with Brian...

"So you hit a girl in the face?"

I feel embarrassed even talking about it.

"It wasn't like a punch or anything."

"So you slapped a girl in the face?" Brian rephrases.

"No, it wasn't exactly a slap either." I pause. "It was like...I pushed her."

"Well, it doesn't matter which hand position you used. What matters was the intent."

I look at Brian, sort of knowing what *intent* means, but sort of not.

"What did she do that made you mad enough to hit her?"

"She just won't ever stop talking and I get sick of it."

"Are you sure that's the reason?"

I think for a second. "I don't know."

"Well, she pushed your buttons. But the reason you hit her isn't because of her. You can't lash out at your parents, you can't lash out at Jake. So it makes sense that you might find control in lashing out at someone else."

And my best friend who keeps flicking the ball past me.

I put my head down. He's right.

I do want to grab my mom or my dad by the ears and scream in their face, but that would be impossible to pull off. I could try it, but they'd probably ground me for twenty-five years and chain me to my desk. And with Jake, if I grabbed him by the ears and screamed in his face, he would grab my arm and twist it behind my back.

"I'm not saying it's true, but does that sound reasonable?"

"Yeah," I say, feeling ashamed.

I look up at Brian, who looks back at me with kindness in his eyes.

I start breathing heavy and my eyes squish together and it's like a volcano inside of me that is going to erupt, I hear the low rumbling and see sparks in front of my squished eyes and the more I try to hold it back the harder it is to stop until finally...

I throw my head down into the couch pillow and scream and scream and scream until my vocal cords feel like shredded chicken. I wait for Brian to kick me out for being so loud, but he doesn't.

This feels like a scene from the zoo when a wild animal starts acting wild and the person at the zoo is eating popcorn and laughing at the animal from outside the cage.

But I glance at Brian and he's not laughing or eating popcorn. He's just watching me and jotting things down in his notebook and letting me get whatever this is out of my system. This must be part of why I'm here, maybe ALL of why I'm here.

It feels good to scream and let it out, but it hurts really bad and my brain throbs and my throat stings.

And then it's over. I lie there with my head on the pillow looking back and forth between the window and Brian, who hasn't taken his eyes off me the whole time.

"I'm proud of you, Benny." He tells me we went over our time, but that it was an important break-through and that I should go home and get some rest.

I sleep for twelve hours straight.

15

Mr. Rodgers asks me to come see him after class. I don't even know what to say. I think he's going to yell at me again or find another drawing in a book, not that I ever did that again.

Standing next to his desk and waiting for all the kids to leave is making me really nervous. He looks at me with his Frankenstein eyes.

"I heard about your father."

I look at him, not knowing how he knows or why he knows.

"I'm so sorry."

I lower my head.

"I hope you aren't embarrassed by me knowing this. I also have a little information about what's going on at home. You know, your mom not being there."

I can't speak.

"Listen, if there's anything I can do to help you…"

And with that, I just start crying. Right there. On the spot. No tissues around, no notepads to write down thoughts, no couch to sit on. No hugs. No anything. It's just me with tears streaming down my face. When I cry, I can't breathe well and when I go to talk it sounds like I'm choking on my own spit.

"I understand, Ben. My life was similar to yours when I was young, so I understand. You can't let it beat you."

"I don't know how to fight," I say.

"You don't need to fight. You need to focus. I can help you."

Nothing can help me. I am beyond help, and plus, I can't even see Mr. Rodgers clearly through my tears. I wipe my eyes on my sleeve, then on the other one.

He reaches into his desk and pulls out a box of tissues.

"Go home and rest, then tomorrow gather all the materials from all your classes. Organize all of it into a space on your desk. For the next week,

when the class is outside for recess, you and I are going to put in some work time. Does that sound okay?"

"Mm-hmm," I say. It seems like something I can do.

It's right around Valentine's Day and even though I know for a fact that Mr. Rodgers isn't my valentine, I feel like there are hearts flying into my chest and filling me up.

When I leave Mr. Rodgers's room, I see Lori out of the corner of my eye. She's coming right at me. She's walking fast, weaving in and out of the crowd with her hands behind her back ready to spring something on me. Oh my gosh. I think she's going to hug me!

She stops right in front of me and her arm swings forward.

She can't stop smiling. Even when she turns to walk away, she is still smiling from ear to ear and watching and waiting for me to open the envelope.

It has a heart on it and smells like fruity perfume. When I open it I see a little bee on the inside.

I do not in any way want to "bee" hers. I guess I could end the whole thing right here and now by tearing up the valentine but I don't have it in me. All I can do is smile back and say thank you.

I go home and rest like Mr. Rodgers said.

I take a shower and get my pajamas on. Then I do a practice run and get all my stuff organized like he suggested. I put pencils in this pile, papers in that one. My books have barely been opened but I stack them, too. Erasers. Notebook paper. It's all here, and everything looks practically brand-new.

What I don't have is a pencil sharpener, and it would be really handy now because a bunch of my pencils have broken tips.

I walk across the hall into Libby's room. I open her desk drawer and start looking for a sharpener.

Nope. Nothing.

I find lots of candy wrappers and notes stuffed in her drawers but no sharpener.

The notes look interesting. It's hard not to be nosy when you see folded-up pieces of paper with handwriting on them. So I open one.

It's got hearts all over it. I get a little grossed out that Libby could be in love with someone.

I fold the note up and put it back in the drawer. She has other drawers in her desk, which could have what I'm looking for, so I look.

Not in that one.

Not in that one either. Wow, she sure eats a lot of candy.

Across the room is her dresser. She's probably not sharpening pencils at her dresser, but it's worth a look.

I walk over and open the top drawer and there's a brush and a comb but also dirty socks and an old teddy bear stuffed in the corner. Even though I can tell right away there are no pencil sharpeners, there is one thing that stands out.

I know I should shut the drawer and walk away but it's hard to see a diary and not want to read it, so I click the little latch on the front and it opens up.

Wow! It's like a treasure chest of fancy writing and hearts and it even smells a little like Lori's fruity valentine. It's hard for me to read girls' handwriting sometimes, but I can make out a bunch of words.

Scott. Kiss. Nice dream.

I flip around and read different entries. In this one she talks about another boy, named Michael, who she thinks is cute. And in this one she talks about her best friend, Chris, and how they stayed up and watched movies one night and painted their nails all glittery. And in this one...

My heart plinks out of my chest as the diary drops from my hands. Libby runs toward me with so much hate in her eyes, I think fireballs are going to come shooting out of them.

"That's private!" She pushes me out of the way.

Libby is mad. Really mad. As she should be.

I hear her running downstairs yelling for Dad so she can tell him that I read her diary, but he must be out somewhere.

I am so stupid. The kind of stupid that never gets smarter. The kind of stupid where one day, I won't even remember my name or how to go to the bathroom anymore. I hope not, but it feels like I'm heading there.

And it makes me realize I have something to take care of that I should have taken care of a while ago. I throw my jacket on and walk to Theo's house.

It's hard making a mistake, then having to go and apologize to someone, even if it's a really, really, really good friend. It actually may be worse if they're a really good friend. When I knock on the front door and Theo answers it instead of his mom, we just look at each other. I say what I need to say:

And he smiles and I know that everything is going to be okay.

Then we ride bikes and I do pretty well, and then we go up into his loft and just keep on being friends, like nothing ever happened.

16

"Mom, why can't you and Dad get back together?"

There's a long pause.

"That's a tough one to answer."

"Why can't you answer my question?"

"I just don't think that would be a good idea. It's complicated, Benny."

Complicated, to me, is a puzzle that has two thousand pieces that takes years to put together.

Mom sighs on the other end of the phone and, in one long monologue, tells a story of all the yelling and all the meanness and all the rest of whatever else they did to each other. Then I sigh, not knowing why I asked that question, but knowing it just came out and I feel a little worse now.

"I wanna talk to Mom," begs Libby. I say goodbye to Mom and hand Libby the phone.

The doctor was right. Dad has gotten a lot worse and it happened really fast. It didn't take long for him to go from coughing blood to not being able to hold himself up.

Now he's in a bed at the hospital and he can't do much at all except watch TV and sleep, depending on how tired he is.

It feels like we sort of live by ourselves now. I say "sort of" because Mom pops in and out and my grandmother comes over and makes sure we're eating and cleaning ourselves and not burning the place down. I guess she and my dad had some sort of fight years ago, but now that Dad has cancer, Grandma comes and helps out with stuff. I imagine that's what family is supposed to do.

She brings food for us but not the kind of food you make meals with. Last week, she brought a giant can of chocolate pudding and big boxes of cereal and a huge block of cheese. The pudding had to be opened with a can opener. Every day after school I'd get out a spoon and squat in front of the fridge and shovel it straight out of the can into my mouth.

GULP!

PUDDING

I did that for a week straight and there was still more than half of it left. The rim had dried pudding around it and it was starting to look a little weird by the end of the week but I didn't care. I also ate a lot of cheese chunks and handfuls of cereal straight from the box.

Grandma doesn't talk much. She makes dinner for us but usually doesn't stay past eight o'clock. Then we're supposed to finish our homework and put ourselves to bed.

It's weird not having Dad in the next room. Strangely, as much as his coughing made my heart skip beats, it was always a signal that he was home.

But even stranger, now that he's not here, I feel a calm come over me and I've been sleeping better and not having to squish my eyes together and try different sleeping positions or lie outside in the cold feeling like I want to explode.

Things have been going pretty smoothly for me. I'm surprisingly focused.

Mr. Rodgers has been helping me get a handle on all my schoolwork. He's actually not a jerk at all. He has a wife and a dog and a one-year-old daughter and he likes to talk about them every chance he gets. They're planning a trip to Hawaii this summer and he's excited.

Visiting Dad in the hospital is weird. First of all, hospitals have an odd smell, like breath mints, Band-Aids, and soap all mixed together, and when you walk in, it's all clean and smooth and shiny and white, just like on TV.

Mom leads Jake, Libby, and me through the front doors, down a hall, up the elevators, and down another hall and around the corner and to another desk, where she tells the nurse who we're here to see.

219

"Oh, him," she says with a smirk on her face. "Now, he's trouble!"

I know she's kidding, but maybe she's not. Dad seems like he could be a lot of trouble.

The nurse grabs a chart and we follow her down the hall and around another corner and down a longer hall until we get to his room.

Room C-346. I think the C stands for *cancer*, since we're in the Cancer Ward.

"There he is!" the nurse says. We all walk into the room and see Dad with a tube up his nose and another tube sticking out of his arm, and he's tucked into his bed wearing a hospital gown. He's also missing his hair and beard. He looks tired but happy to see us.

His voice is raspy and weak.

I look around. The TV is on and he's watching some game show and it's kind of loud, but the nurse reaches up and turns the volume down a little. There are two beds in the room, but the one that Dad isn't in is empty. There's a cafeteria tray with his lunch on it and I wonder what's on the plate under the aluminum foil.

That was Harry's bed.
He left yesterday.

I wonder for a second if he left the room or if he left Earth.

"He was a nice guy. We didn't talk much, but he had a good sense of humor about the whole thing."

I guess "had" means that Harry died.

Mom sits down next to the window and looks outside, then back at us now and again.

"Thanks for bringing the kids, Jo."

Dad calls her Jo, short for Joanne. He's trying to be nice despite the situation but she's in a more serious mood.

"You're welcome. How are you feeling?"

"Okay. Except these tubes are a pain in the neck. And the arm. And the leg."

No one laughs.

"So, kids, how's Grandma treating you?"

"Good, I guess," mumbles Jake.

"Fine," says Libby.

"She brings over giant cans of pudding and tons of cheese," I say.

"Ha. That's Grandma for you," Dad jokes.

Then we all sit there. Mom reads while the rest of us watch TV.

After a while, I walk up to Dad's bed and look at the tube coming out of his arm and at all the machinery hooked up to him. He looks really tired and like he wants to fall asleep but is trying hard to look strong for us.

He grabs my hand.

"Hey," he says. I look up at him.

Things are going to be okay.

He squeezes my hand like he's juicing a lemon, and I look back at him wanting to say *I know,* but not really sure if that's true.

I have his attention, which is hard to get, and it's funny how ideas flash into your mind. I think about us going bowling like he always said we might do.

So instead of asking him again now and knowing what the answer would be, I get a better idea. I run out of the room to the nurses' desk.

A nurse named Kathy finds six tubes of lip balm for me, and I take them back into Dad's room. Then

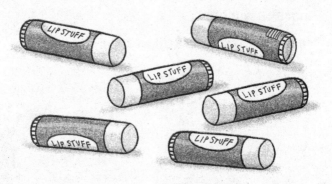

I pull the aluminum foil off the lunch plate, which uncovers half-eaten lasagna of all things, and roll the foil into a ball.

"What the heck are you doing?" Jake asks.

"You'll see," I say, focused on my work.

I empty the rolling tray next to Dad's bed and set up the lip balm tubes. Then I hand the aluminum-foil ball to Dad.

Dad looks at the mini bowling alley, then at me. He seems embarrassed that he never made good on his promise to take me bowling, but it doesn't matter anymore.

We play Lip Balm Bowling for the next hour and everyone laughs and nobody fights and nobody throws the lasagna against the wall or shouts or anything. Once again we are a family, even if it's only for an hour, and it makes me happy.

17

"Okay, let's start!" yells Theo as Brooke and Emily face off in the center of the cul-de-sac, click sticks, and go after the ball. Brooke gets the ball first and whizzes around, then passes the ball to Cole.

"Nice pass, Brooke!" And then he whizzes it back to Theo, but not before I jut my stick out and block the pass.

Now I have the ball and I'm feeling pretty good. I'm as focused as I can be. I take the ball and zigzag through everyone, even though I'm supposed to be on defense.

Out of the blue, Theo shoves his stick in my path and knocks the ball to Brooke, who passes the ball back to Theo, who's barreling past me. He takes the ball and I suddenly get a burst of energy that goes right down into my legs. Theo loses the ball as it bounces off the edge of the manhole cover and out of reach. That gives me time to get back on defense and then...I wait for him to come.

He dribbles the ball in my direction and I can tell in his eyes that he wants to do the flick shot. Without missing a beat, Theo dribbles up and gets ready to shoot.

I am ready, too.

I wait for it. Then he does a stutter step and I put my stick out.

At the last second...

He flicks it.

And I try not to lunge too far forward even though it's hard to stop your own weight once you've started. But I pull my stick up into the air and...

CRACK!

The ball hits my stick.

And in what seems like slow motion, it flies off behind Theo and rolls toward the goal. Emily gets it and, with a little flick move of her own, scores.

"Oh my gosh. It's a miracle," Theo says.

He looks at me with a half smile and I look at him back with a full one and we high-five and keep on playing.

Even though I may have beat Theo's flick shot, I'm finding it a little harder to succeed elsewhere. It's getting a tiny bit easier to focus, and Mr. Rodgers has really helped me to organize better. I mean, I got a C the other day on a math test, which is an improvement. And I've actually been doing my homework at home, which is something to be proud of, I guess. At least Mr. Rodgers is proud of me.

Dad is getting worse. We see him every few days and also talk to him on the phone. Grandma keeps bringing giant cans of food for us and we keep eating them. She's starting to get a little nicer toward us, which is good because playing games with a grumpy person is the worst.

YOU CHEATED!

Now this sounds like one of those sequences from a movie where the narrator has to fit all the things that have happened into a short block of time, but that's kind of how things have gone.

I'm not happy and I'm not sad, I'm just here, try-ing to keep from failing school, actually getting some sleep at night, and maybe for once in a long time feeling less angry.

The biggest thing is that Dad wants to die at home. The hospital people set up a bed in the living room so Dad doesn't have to go up and down the stairs anymore, and now we see him right when we come home from school.

He just lies in his bed in the front of the house and shouts things to us like:

I need some water!

He's not mean about it, he just can't get it himself.

Mom has been coming over to help, too. Mom and Grandma don't get along too well, because I guess they both want to do the talking, but now that Dad's days are fewer I think they're doing their best to be nice to each other. They normally get into arguments about things like curtain colors. One time they had an argument about how to cook a roast. It was as if they were going to jump up and start punching each other like boxers.

But now they just sit and look into the distance like they're both trying not to cry and I definitely know what that's like. Most of the time, it's a lot better to cry it out than to have it sit inside and make you mad, or sick, or not be able to sleep.

Grandma kisses Dad goodbye, then hugs all of us and leaves.

Mom takes over the talking and I just shake my head because when Mom gets yakking she yaks and yaks and can't really slow herself down. I leave and go up to my room. Then I realize I left my backpack downstairs in the living room and when I go down to get it, I stop in my tracks.

Mom and Dad are hugging like I've never seen people hug before and they're crying and whispering words to each other and I can't hear what they're saying, but it seems kind.

Then I stand right there and start thinking. I think of all the times I watched them fight and heard them argue and yell and all of the smoke and not going bowling and not getting my bike and Jake spitting on me and me snooping around Libby's room. All those thoughts come to me at once and I don't feel like crying about it and I'm not

squishing my eyes together and my blood isn't rushing into my hands and I don't feel like screaming. It all just comes in, then goes out, and I breathe.

Then I come out of my daydream and Mom is standing right in front of me.

Hey, handsome.

"I'm going to leave now."

Normally I don't know what to say, but today, while I stand on the stairs, something comes to me.

"Thank you for hugging Dad, even though I know you don't love him anymore."

Mom sighs, but with a smile, and looks back at Dad, who is smiling, too.

I go outside and lie in the grass. Looking up at the sky, as clouds pass by, I wonder where Dad is headed. I wonder if there really is a place where you can go and not have anything bother you ever again. I wonder if he'll end up there.

18

I've never had to work so hard in my life. Just doing all my homework is bad enough, but to keep myself focused and help my dad and watch him fall asleep some nights and keep Grandma off my back about everything—it's plenty.

Brian has been helping me get a lot of this out, and Mr. Rodgers has really helped me get a handle on all my homework and tests and stuff. When I think of them both and all they do for me, I feel grateful.

People have been coming in and out of the house for weeks now. Many of them are from Dad's work, and a couple of neighbors have visited, too. What's weird is that a lot of Dad's old friends from high school are coming by, and I've not seen or heard of any of them before. They never came around when Dad wasn't sick, but now they all want to see him for the last time.

It's actually really sad to watch them come and spend a few minutes with Dad, then leave with their hats in their hands.

Grandma has been staying over a lot. She goes to bed early and gets up early, and some mornings she actually makes pancakes and bacon for us.

Jake and Libby and I look up at Grandma cutting her bacon and wonder what she means by that.

"He just never got around to taking care of himself. His health, his home, his relationships, his kids. He deserves everything he gets. Even this."

That was a mean thing to say, but I think Grandma may have hit it right on the head.

Dad never did take care of things. I mean, he lived in the house with us, but even when he was here, he wasn't ever really HERE. The backyard was a mess, dinners were never really planned, milk got sour, he couldn't quit smoking, and all kinds of other stuff.

I take my plate up to the sink and rinse it off. The water coming out of the faucet is the only sound I can hear in this quiet house.

We all go into the living room and gather around Dad, who's been sleeping for a couple of days. We've been watching him get worse and now when he's awake he can barely speak. He's gotten really skinny and pale and we can see veins in his arms. It's like he's disappearing right before our eyes.

Some hospital people have been coming in daily to check on him. The rest of the time, it's just us.

Grandma walks over and pulls the top of the blanket up to Dad's chin, like she's tucking him in. He looks like a child lying there. It gives me an idea.

I run upstairs to my room and bring down Stuffed Raccoon and lay him down next to Dad. Then I pull the blanket up over them both.

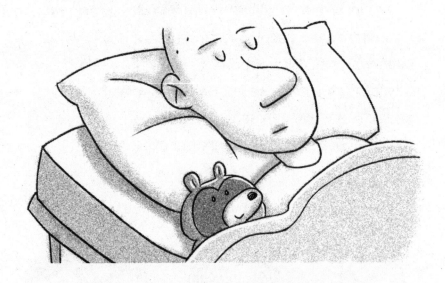

I never did give Stuffed Raccoon a real name. There weren't any good ones that stood out.

But right now, in this moment, the perfect name comes to mind.

Buddy.

It seems like a common name for a stuffed animal but he is my buddy and now he can be Dad's buddy because Dad needs comfort more than anyone I know.

Grandma takes me to Brian's the next day, and he and I just sit and talk, not about me so much.

"How is everything, Ben?"

"Okay, I guess. Dad doesn't wake up anymore and he's probably going to die soon."

Brian lets out a long sigh. He looks out the window.

Then he takes my hand.

Promise me you'll keep going.

"Keep going where?"

"When you're feeling that feeling that takes you over and makes you want to squish your eyes and scream, just keep going and push through that."

I look down at the floor and wonder if I have it in me to keep going. I decide that I do.

"I will," I say, and I believe it.

Brian and I give each other a long hug.

Later in the day, I get the news that I passed the fifth grade, which is one of the biggest miracles of my life. Not only have I avoided being Libby's dumb, flunky brother, I actually feel as if a dark cloud has lifted off me.

Mr. Rodgers sees me in the hall.

Maybe I am. But I really don't know.

Then he says, "Once you realize how much you have to give, which is a lot, you're going to soar."

I look at Mr. Rodgers and think of flying into the clouds and getting away from it all, but then wonder if that might just be everyone's goal — to do so well that you can do anything you want.

At the end of the day, I see Lori. She's standing there as I walk down the hall and she smiles. The more I walk, the more she stares, and it dawns on me that I might be able to end this once and for all.

So without breaking stride I walk right up to her with my arms extended. As I get closer she starts to get a terrified look on her face. I hold my arms out like a zombie and say:

And I wrap my arms around her shoulders.

"Ewww! Get away!" She pushes her way out of my zombie grasp and runs down the hall.

"Weirdo!" she calls back.

And that is that.

I also found out that Krista is moving to another town this summer so there'll be no more staring over at her in class and dreaming about her long shiny hair.

I leave school feeling good and get on the bus. The whole ride home I hear Betsy yak-yak-yakking and all I can do is laugh to myself. Then I turn around.

So what are you girls talking about? It sounds Sooooo INTERESTING!

"Leave us alone...Benjamin."

And we smile fake smiles at each other.

At night, I'm dreaming of driving on a long empty road and I'm driving and driving and all of a sudden I see a brick wall in the distance and it's getting closer and closer and closer and I'm just about to hit it when…

I wake up.

I hear some shuffling around downstairs so I get out of bed to go see what's happening. I hear Grandma sniffling and when I get to the bottom of the stairs I see her across the room holding Dad's hand and rubbing it softly.

I walk down the rest of the stairs and across the floor quietly like I don't want to wake Dad up, which seems silly because he isn't going to.

I stand there and stare at him, then at Grandma, then back at Dad.

Grandma leans down and kisses Dad on the forehead.

From there, it's all just a blur of Libby and Jake waking up and Mom coming over and the hospital people swarming the house and at some point everyone leaves and I'm the only one sitting there in the living room with Dad. Then a couple of men come in and take Dad's body and put it into a big bag that's the same length as he is. Then they carry him out.

Then it's just me. I'm not numb and not mad and not sad. I get up and walk outside and stand on the porch behind Mom with my hands on her shoulders. Jake and Libby come over and sit on each side of her and we all watch everything play out. They put Dad into an ambulance and at some point everyone is gone. I look up at the sky, and clouds pass by, and I wonder if I'll be able to keep going like I promised Brian or even soar like Mr. Rodgers said.

"I guess we just have to keep going, huh, kids?"
Mom says, and I stand over her, looking out into
the air.

19

There is nothing on my mind as we drive to the funeral home. All I can hear is my own heartbeat and the slapping sound of Jake playing air drums on his thighs. Libby is humming to herself. It sounds like a lullaby but if I listen harder, it's just a lot of random notes.

I look at the back of Mom's head as she drives. She turns the car left. She steps on the brakes. She steps on the gas. She turns the car right. Over and over. She takes in a deep breath and then sighs it out.

I hear the tires roll across the gravel driveway and we pull into a space close to the entrance of the funeral home. We pile out of the car and into the haze of the air and the brightness of the sky.

It smells like rain.

We walk toward the door—Mom, Libby, Jake, then me. When we get inside, it feels like the lobby of a wax museum. It smells like wax, too. I take a seat next to Libby as Jake sits down in a chair across the room.

An old man appears and walks over to Mom.

"I'm sorry for your loss, Mrs. Brooks."

"I'm not his wife," Mom says.

"Understood. Here is the paperwork we'll need you to sign."

She takes the papers, looks at them for a moment, and just sits there, in deep thought.

The old man turns to me, Jake, and Libby.

"Would any of you like one last goodbye?" the old man asks. "We've made a one-time concession, courtesy of your grandmother."

There's silence. A fire truck screams by outside and then fades away.

Mom shifts in her seat. "That won't be necessary."

I glare at Mom and try to speak up, but no words come out. I look at Libby for some help, then Jake. They both seem to be in their own worlds, staring at their hands and nervously tapping their feet.

Then I look at the man, who's been watching me the whole time.

He nods a silent yes with his head.

Mom, Jake, and Libby all snap to attention as I stand up and walk toward the man.

"Right this way, son."

Every one of my steps feels like I'm wearing cement shoes, but with all the courage I can gather, I put one foot in front of the other and follow the man behind the curtain and into the darkness.

The second set of curtains opens in front of me and it's like walking into a weird science-fiction movie with the tile floor, white walls, and fluorescent lights buzzing above. There are no test tubes, or laser scalpels, but there is a figure in the middle of the room on a table and it isn't an alien in a jar.

Dad is white as a sheet, just like the one that's covering him from his chest to his ankles. He's still bald, just like he'd been throughout chemotherapy, but maybe a little balder.

"Will ten minutes be enough time?" the old man asks.

I look at him and nod.

Seeing Dad lying there reminds me of seeing him in a deep sleep on the couch or in bed. Sometimes I would just stare at him and wonder what it would be like to see him dead. Now, strangely, I am looking at him dead and wondering if he is actually asleep instead. His lungs are not going up and down and I've never seen him so still.

I walk around him, mesmerized by how quiet he is.

I get up close to his face and stare at him.

My eyes start to burn, first from concentration, then slowly from the tears that are building up.

I lean in close, pause for what seems like a week, then close my eyes and kiss him on the forehead.

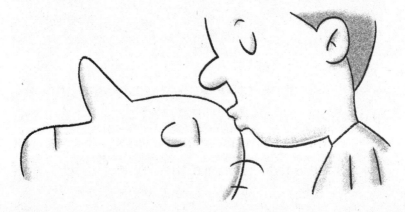

Although my ten minutes with Dad aren't up, this is the last time I'm going to see him and I can't pull my eyes away.

I walk backward, staring at his face the whole time, saying goodbye with my eyes, then slip past the curtains into the lobby.

Mom stands under the porch awning of the funeral home entrance and glares at the pouring rain.

I hope they get his ashes to us soon.

It's like she's talking to the sky and the sky alone.

I step out from under the awning into the rain and start walking toward the car. Mom, Jake, and

Libby are too afraid to get wet, so they hang out in the entryway. It feels good to have the rain on my face. I kick a rock, which almost hits our car, and it bounces to the bottom of a grassy hill. So I walk that way.

"Benny, where are you going?" Mom shouts, but I don't answer.

I hike to the top of the hill and look to the sky. Then I just stand there, with the rain and wind hitting my face. My eyes are shut and the rain picks up, stinging my cheeks with each drop.

I open my eyes and look up at the clouds. They're dark and moving quickly across the sky and even though so much has happened, I wonder at this moment why it feels so good to be alive. A giant wave of joy washes over me and at some point, I can't tell the difference between the raindrops and my tears. I spread out my arms one last time and take it all in.

"Come on, Ben!" shouts Jake. "Get in the car!"

I spin around. My family is looking up at me from the car and for an instant, it gives me hope.

As we drive off, I look out the window and take in the sound of the beating windshield wipers. No one says a word.

I feel Libby take my hand and put it around hers.

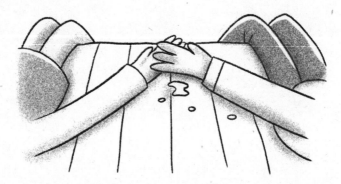

I look over but she's staring out the window humming a lullaby to herself. Jake is air drumming on his legs, but he looks back at me and smiles.

"You look like a wet rat," he says.

Mom looks forward and drives. Raising us by herself wasn't something she planned on, but I'm sure she'll adjust, just like the rest of us.

Mom looks back at me in the rearview mirror and laughs.

"You do look like a wet rat."

And the windshield wipers beat on *THUMP, THUMP, THUMP* just like my heart.

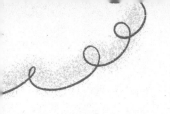

After a few minutes of driving in the rain and listening to some light rock music that Mom likes, I see Jake reaching for the radio knob.

Mom brushes away his hand. "That's my favorite song."

I look at Mom in the rearview mirror, and she winks and puts her arm around Jake. Then she sets her eyes on the road ahead.

As we keep driving, it's quiet and somber, and when the rain finally lets up, there's a sense of calm.

Libby finally lets go of my hand and wipes it on her shirt to dry it off. I'm starting to shiver from my wet clothes.

Mom breaks the silence.

"This is going to take some time to work through, but for now, you'll be staying in your house and I'll be coming to live with you. I can rent out the other place. That's one good thing your dad did early on—invest in that property."

I had no idea that they owned Mom's place. Jake, Libby, and I all look at one another and shrug. Well, at least we'll get the Mexican pot back.

"Oh," continues Mom, "be prepared to have a garage sale."

A garage sale. Hmm. I guess that'll give me a chance to get rid of the stuff I don't need anymore. Jake will probably sell the album he got for Christmas.

We are driving through the neighborhood. Being close to home feels different now that Dad isn't going to be here. A little space inside of me saw this coming but I could never really put it into words.

Hopefully Mom will let us keep on the air-conditioning when it's hot out. And maybe we can get a dog again. Those would be two big improvements.

I look out the window and see our neighbors. Now that the rain has stopped, they're out walking their dogs, getting their mail, and sweeping their garages. Everything seems normal.

But none of these people knows that my dad just died. They'll go on with their lives. And when a family member of theirs dies, I won't hear about it. It's strange how that works.

We keep driving and I see us getting close to where Theo lives. I wonder what he's up to today. He's probably helping his dad fix the car or practicing his flick shot in the garage, just to make sure I never block it again.

As we drive by his house, I see him standing out in his front yard, helping his mom plant some flowers. He looks up and right at me as we drive by and waves a wave that says, *I'm sorry about your dad.*

I wave back.

It's good to have friends. Especially ones who can understand you without even having to say words.

As Theo fades in the distance, Mom turns right, then right again, and pulls up in front of our house.

We all pile out of the car. I look up and the clouds have passed. The clear blue sky is shining.

Then I look down at the street and see a worm. He's alive and plump, slinking toward the grass with his whole life ahead of him, and that makes me smile.

"Ooh, a package!" Libby yells.

"Yeah, and it's big!" Jake says.

I look toward the front door and there's a big brown box sitting there.

I run up to see what it is and look at the address label. It's addressed to me.

Jake starts tearing off the cardboard.

"OUCH!" he screams as he pokes his finger on a staple.

"Serves you right," Mom says. "Let Benny open it. It's for him."

I look at Mom and smile. Then I run into the garage where the toolbox is. I grab a utility knife.

When I get back to the front door, Jake is standing in my way.

"You're so lucky," he says.

And when I look past him, I see that he couldn't resist tearing more of the box open.

What I see is happiness.

And gratitude.

Together.

My heart starts beating out of my chest.

It's brand-new, shiny, and gleaming like nothing I've ever seen before.

I look closer and there's a tag hanging off the handlebars.

I look at Mom and she smiles.

Then I look back at the tag, then back at the bike, then think of the funeral home, and it hits me.

Dad was listening all along.

"How come I didn't get a bike?" Jake asks.

"Not now, Jake," Mom says.

"Ride it, Benny! Ride it!" yells Libby.

I grab the bike by the handlebars, mount the seat, and push off, rolling slowly down the front yard and into the street.

I do some loop-de-loops and then some figure eights and normally, this is where I might start to cry.

But it feels like there are no tears left.

There is only the wind blowing against my face. I decide that I might keep riding forever—to school, to Theo's, maybe even to heaven.

I just keep going, down the street and back again, then around the corner and out of sight. I should probably plan on being back for dinner, because if I'm being honest, Mom does make the best gravy.

A Note from the Author

This is a story close to my heart. It is based on my own childhood growing up in the 1970s at a time when norms associated with parenting and school life were somewhat different than they are today. Divorce, anger issues, my dad's smoking, and his eventual cancer and death impacted my life in a huge way. I tried my best to navigate these waters when I was young and came to rely on the help of others to get me through. If you are struggling in any way, make sure you talk to someone about it—a parent, a teacher, a friend. Help is closer than you think.

The author (left) with his brother and sister in the 1970s.

ETHAN LONG

is the acclaimed author and illustrator of many books for kids, including the Theodor Seuss Geisel Award–winning *Up, Tall and High!* He is also the creator of the Emmy-nominated online series *Scribbles and Ink. The Death and Life of Benny Brooks* is Ethan's first book for older readers and is based on his childhood. He lives with his family in Colorado and invites you to visit him at ethanlong.com.

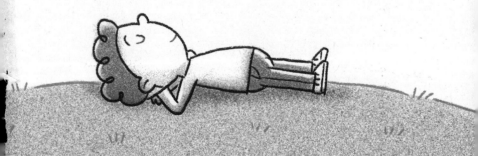